FAR OUT
FAIRY TALES

STONE ARCH BOOKS
a capstone imprint

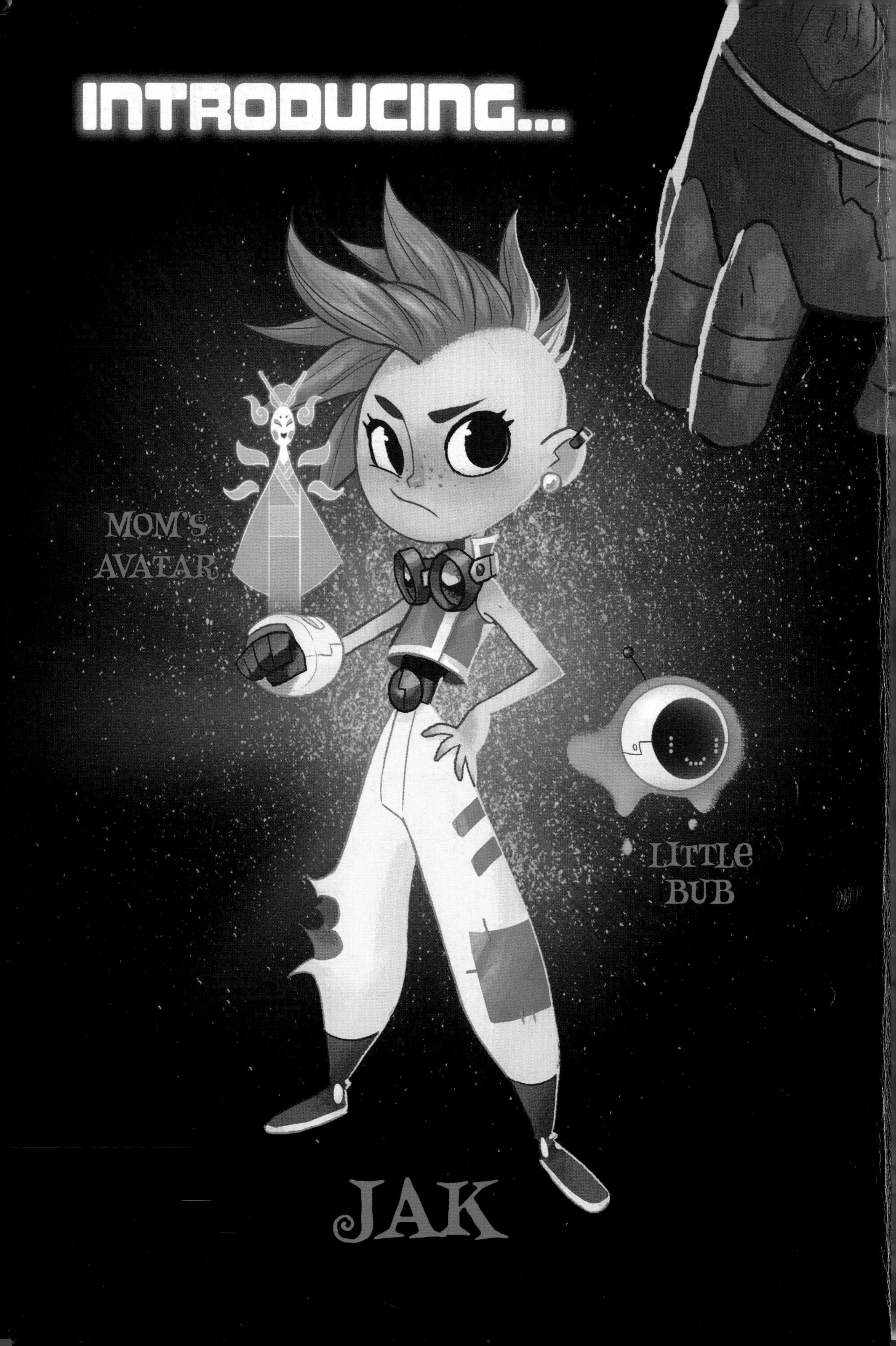
INTRODUCING...
MOM'S AVATAR
LITTLE BUB
JAK

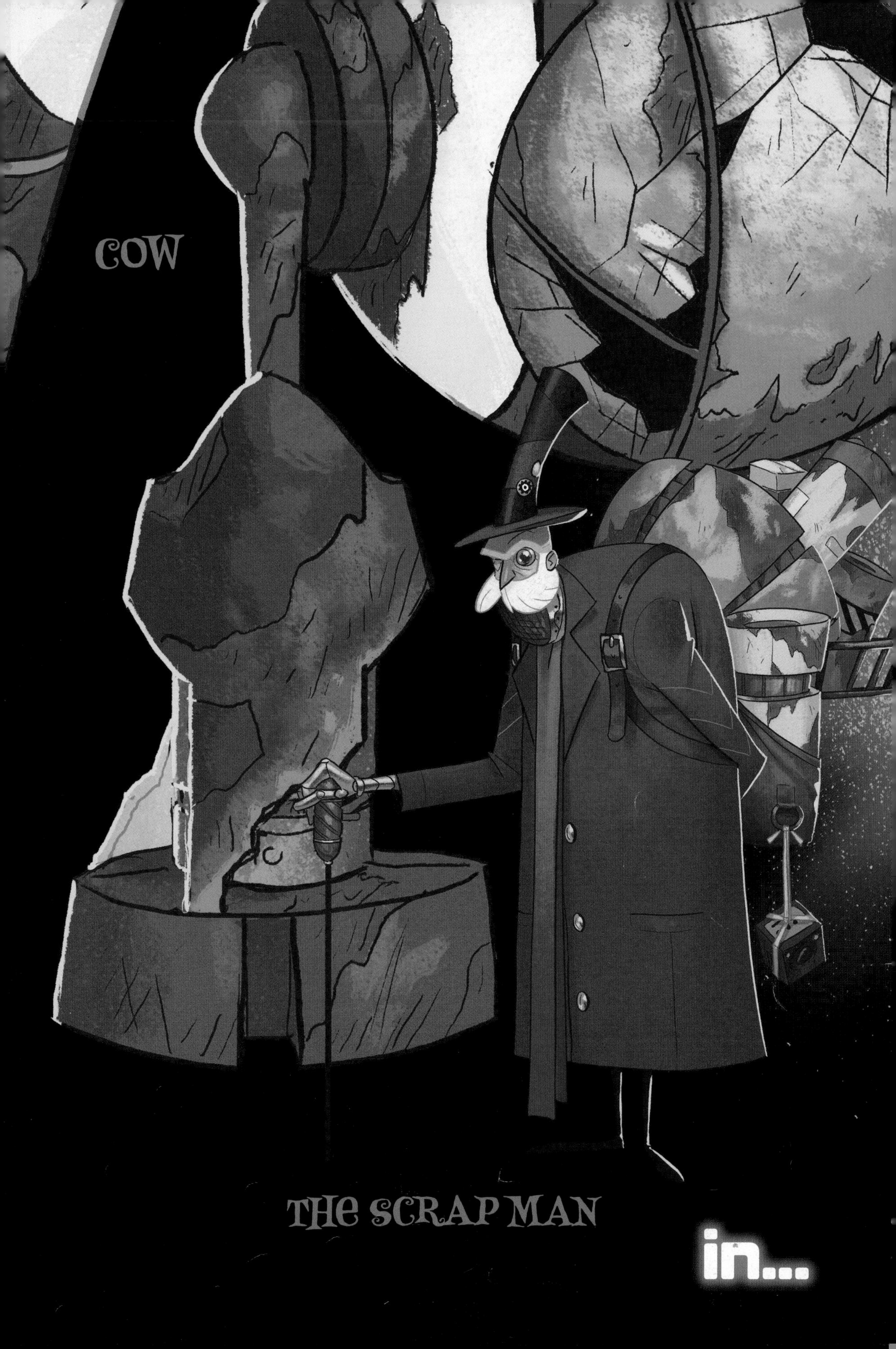
COW
THE SCRAP MAN
in...

Far Out Fairy Tales is published by
Stone Arch Books
A Capstone Imprint
1710 Roe Crest Drive, North Mankato,
Minnesota 56003
www.mycapstone.com

Cataloging-in-Publication Data is
available at the Library of Congress
website.
ISBN 978-1-4965-2510-9 (hardcover)
ISBN 978-1-4965-3117-9 (paperback)
ISBN 978-1-4965-2513-0 (eBook PDF)

Summary: Jak and her robotic
servant, Cow, are in a pickle. Mom
wants Jak to sell Cow for scrap,
but Cow and Jak have become best
friends. So instead of selling the rusty
old robot, Jak strikes a bargain with
the scrap man: if Jak and Cow can
visit the Cloud Kingdom and get hold
of some magic nano-beans, Jak can
keep Cow safe and sound . . .

Designed by Hilary Wacholz
Edited by Sean Tulien
Lettering by Jaymes Reed

Printed in US.
102017 010892R

FAR OUT FAIRY TALES

JAK
AND THE MAGIC
NANO-BEANS

A GRAPHIC NOVEL

BY CARL BOWEN
ILLUSTRATED BY OMAR LOZANO

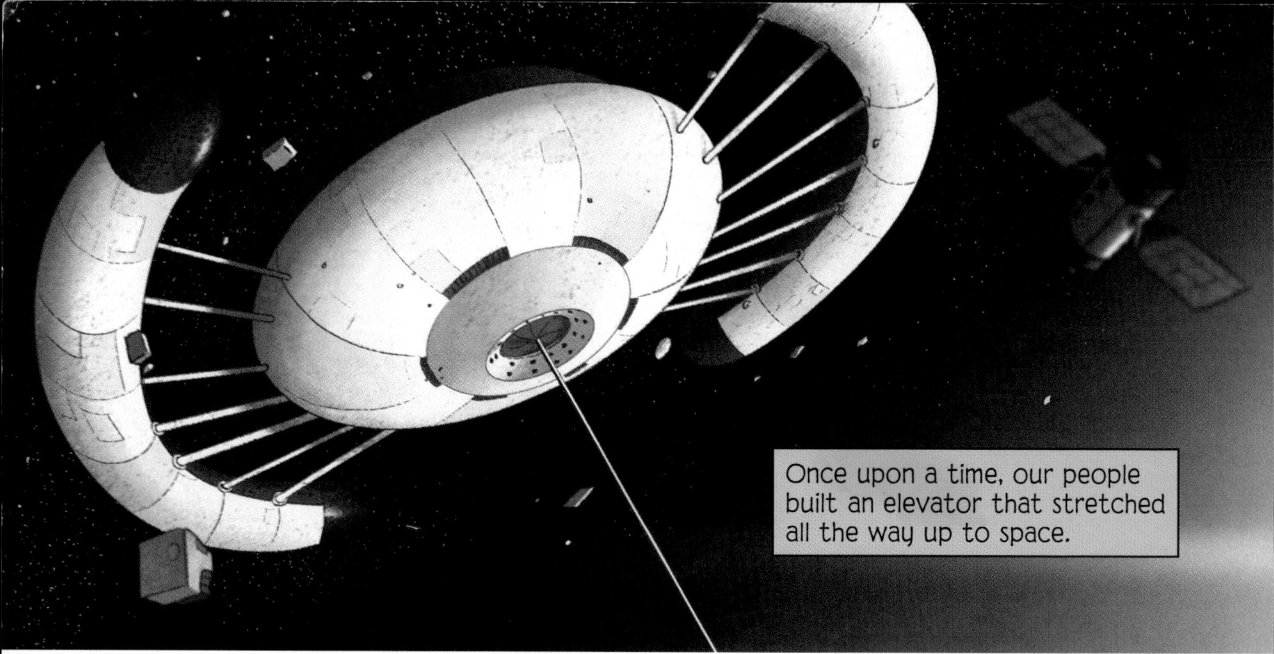
Once upon a time, our people built an elevator that stretched all the way up to space.

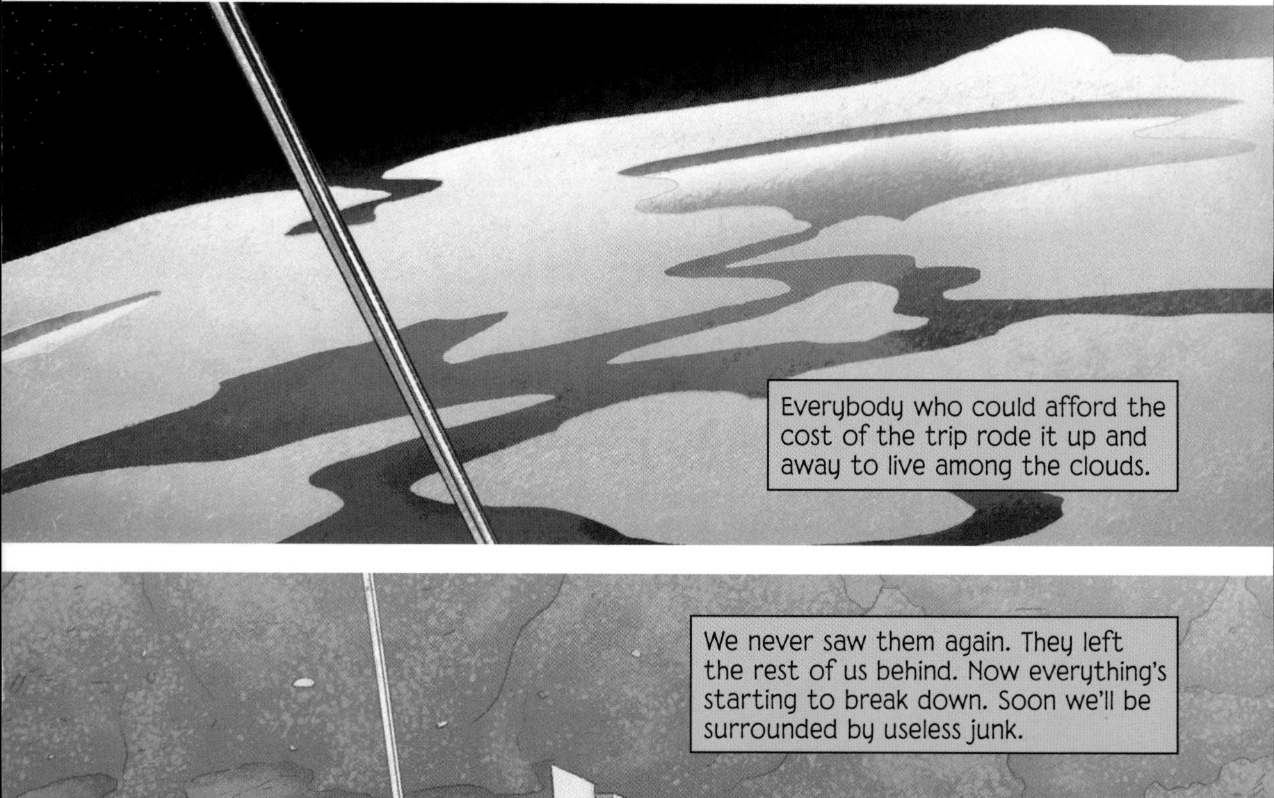
Everybody who could afford the cost of the trip rode it up and away to live among the clouds.

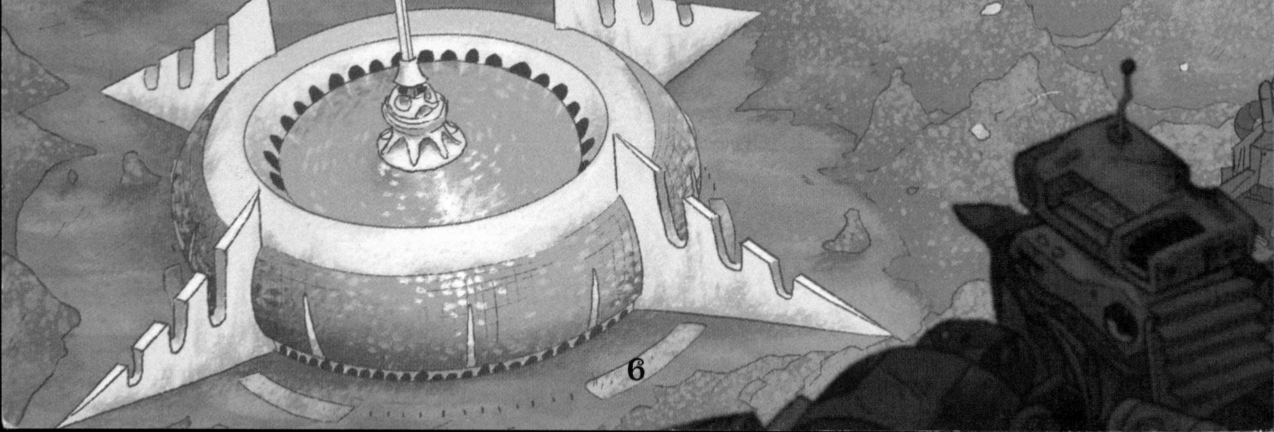
We never saw them again. They left the rest of us behind. Now everything's starting to break down. Soon we'll be surrounded by useless junk.

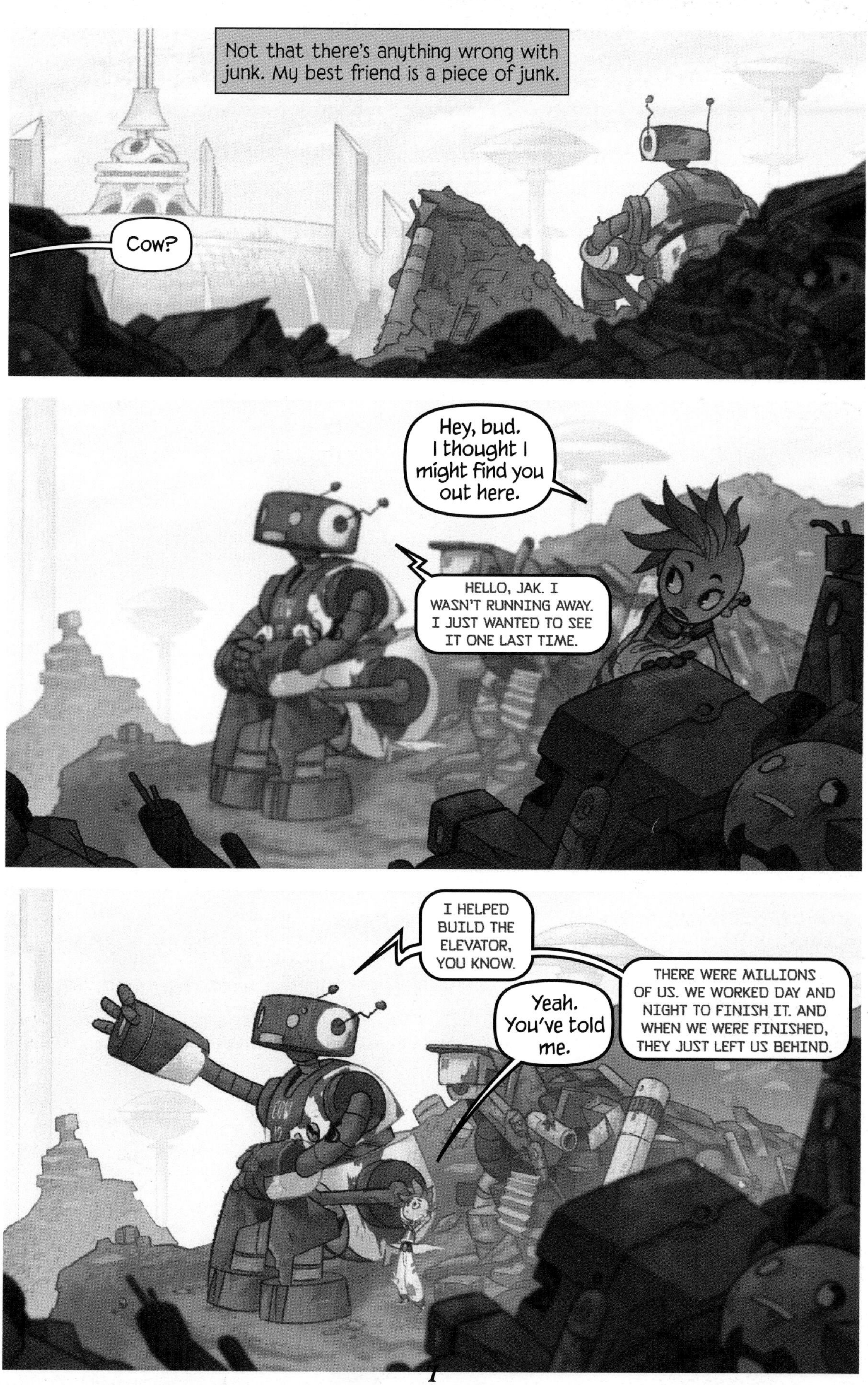
Not that there's anything wrong with junk. My best friend is a piece of junk.
Cow?
Hey, bud. I thought I might find you out here.
HELLO, JAK. I WASN'T RUNNING AWAY. I JUST WANTED TO SEE IT ONE LAST TIME.
I HELPED BUILD THE ELEVATOR, YOU KNOW.
THERE WERE MILLIONS OF US. WE WORKED DAY AND NIGHT TO FINISH IT. AND WHEN WE WERE FINISHED, THEY JUST LEFT US BEHIND.
Yeah. You've told me.

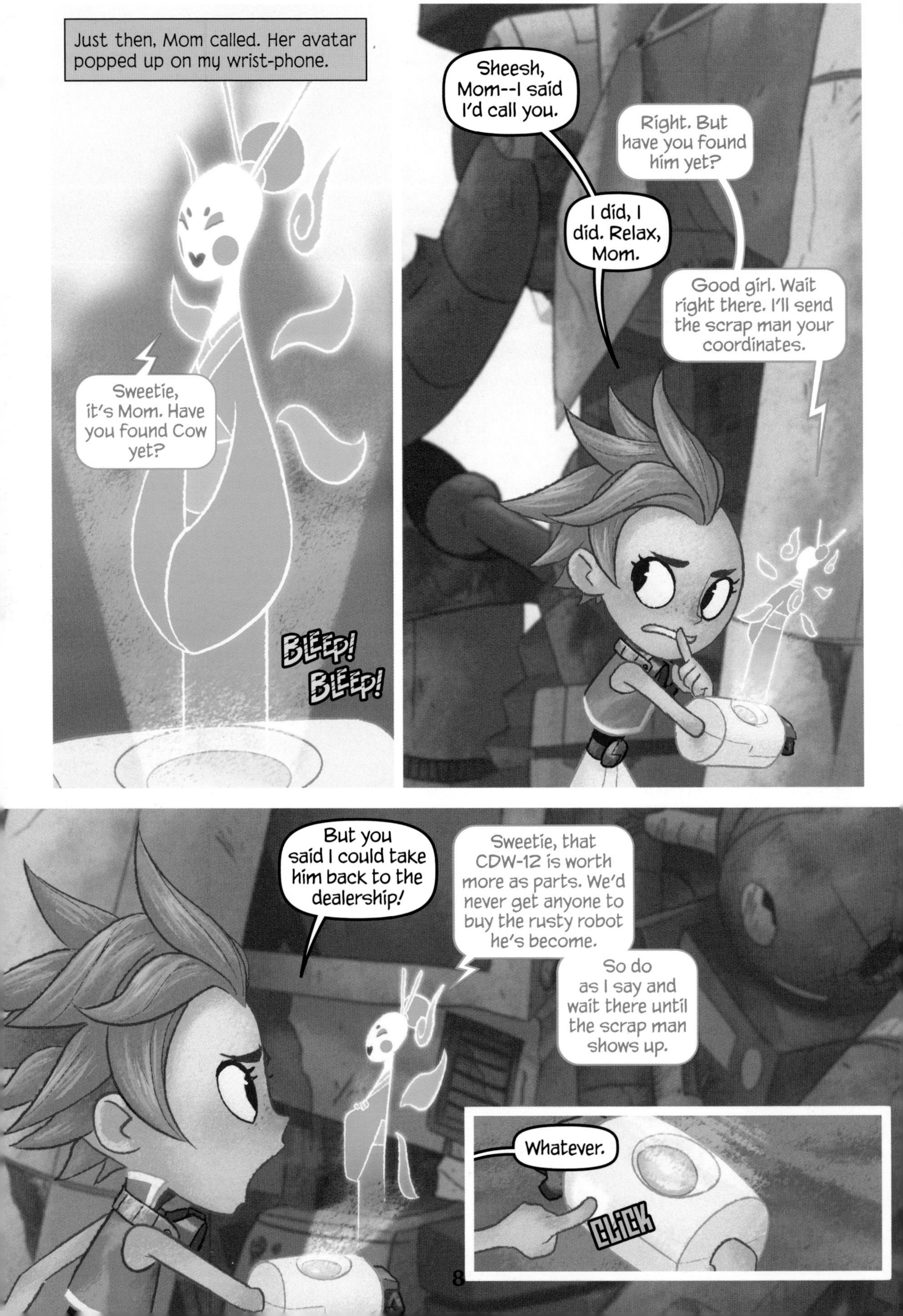

Just then, Mom called. Her avatar popped up on my wrist-phone.
Sweetie, it's Mom. Have you found Cow yet?
BLEEP! BLEEP!
Sheesh, Mom--I said I'd call you.
Right. But have you found him yet?
I did, I did. Relax, Mom.
Good girl. Wait right there. I'll send the scrap man your coordinates.
But you said I could take him back to the dealership!
Sweetie, that CDW-12 is worth more as parts. We'd never get anyone to buy the rusty robot he's become.
So do as I say and wait there until the scrap man shows up.
Whatever.
CLICK

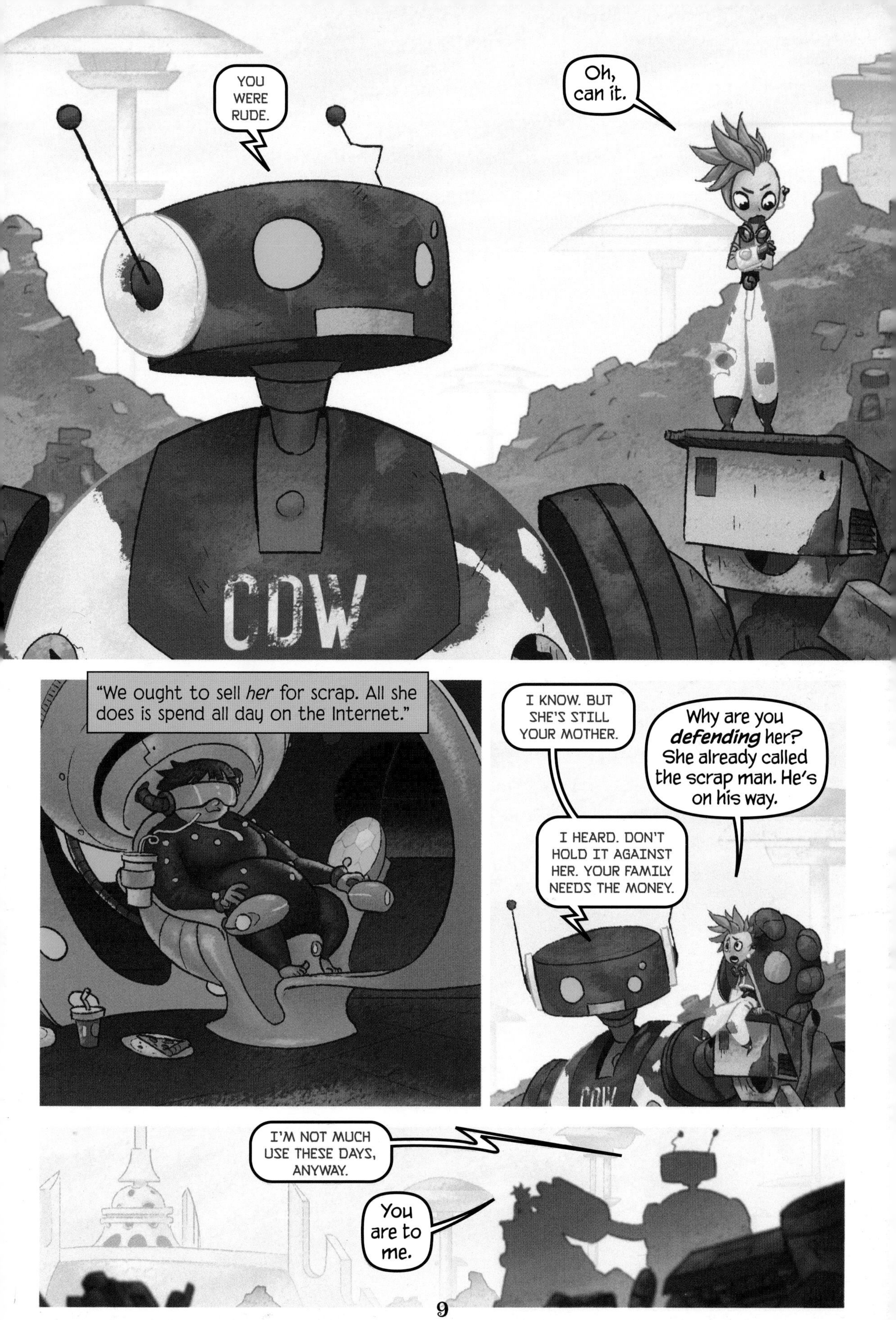
YOU WERE RUDE.
Oh, can it.
COW
"We ought to sell *her* for scrap. All she does is spend all day on the Internet."
I KNOW. BUT SHE'S STILL YOUR MOTHER.
Why are you **defending** her? She already called the scrap man. He's on his way.
I HEARD. DON'T HOLD IT AGAINST HER. YOUR FAMILY NEEDS THE MONEY.
I'M NOT MUCH USE THESE DAYS, ANYWAY.
You are to me.

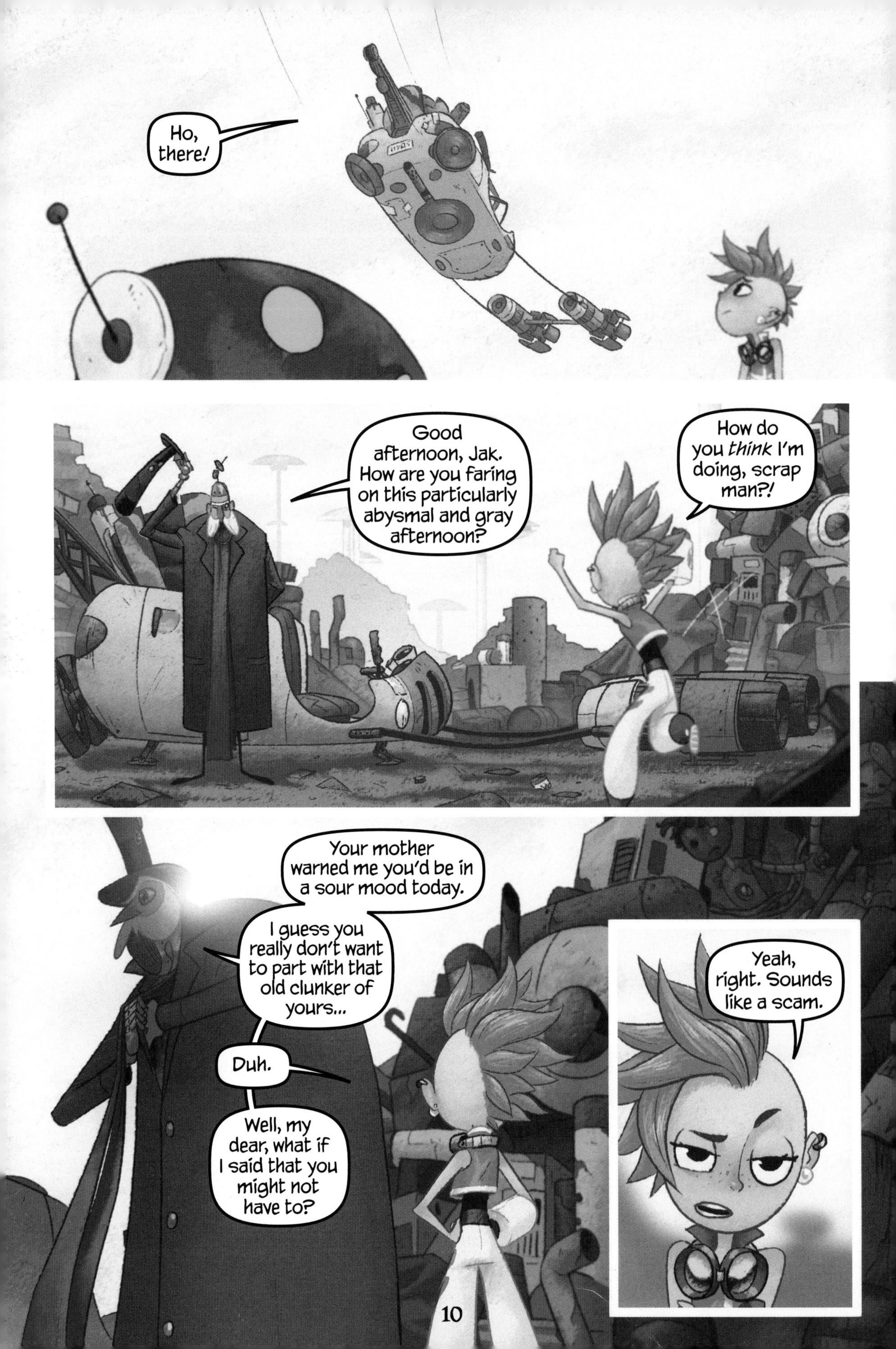
Ho, there!
Good afternoon, Jak. How are you faring on this particularly abysmal and gray afternoon?
How do you *think* I'm doing, scrap man?!
Your mother warned me you'd be in a sour mood today.
I guess you really don't want to part with that old clunker of yours...
Duh.
Well, my dear, what if I said that you might not have to?
Yeah, right. Sounds like a scam.

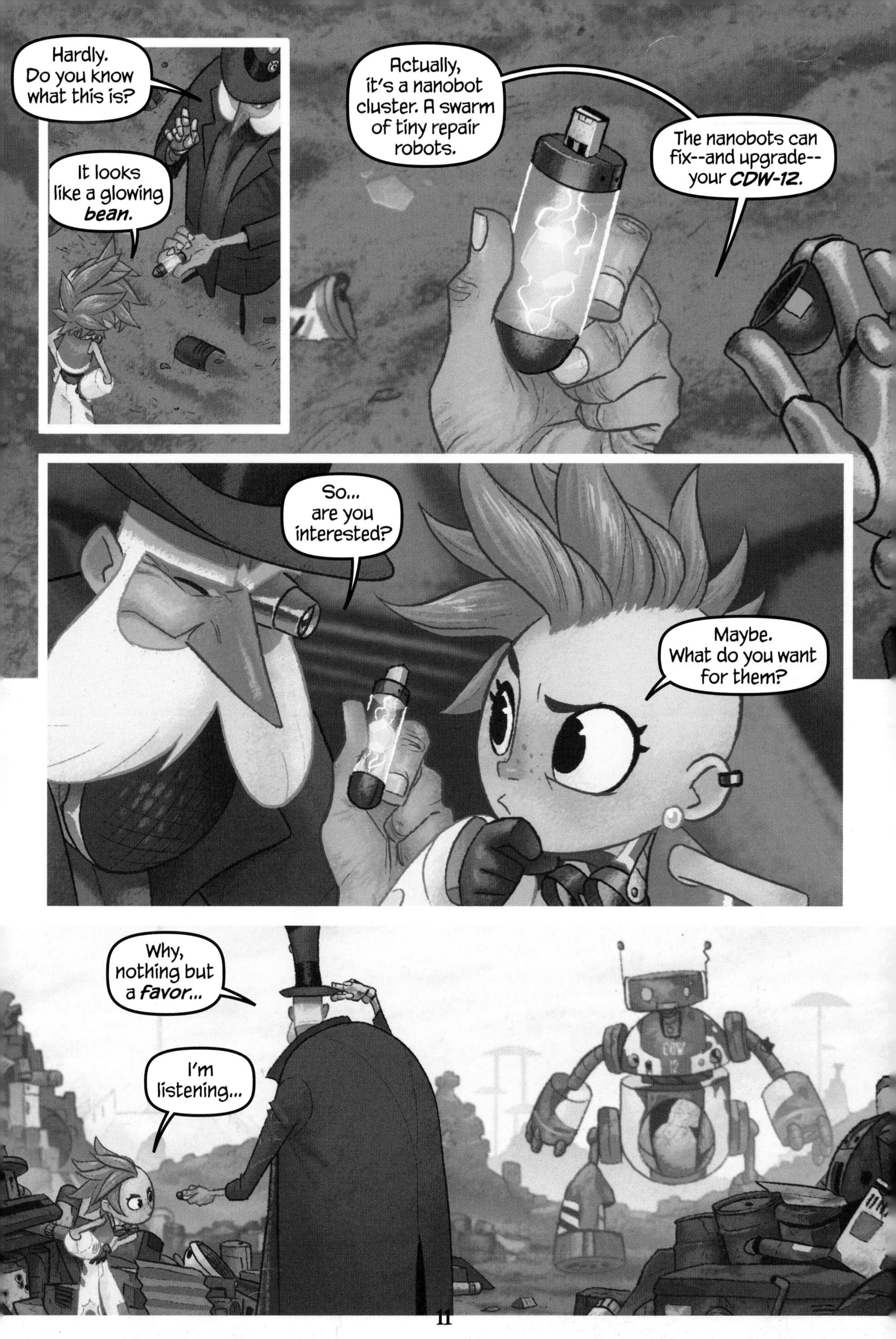
Hardly. Do you know what this is?
It looks like a glowing *bean.*
Actually, it's a nanobot cluster. A swarm of tiny repair robots.
The nanobots can fix--and upgrade--your *CDW-12.*
So... are you interested?
Maybe. What do you want for them?
Why, nothing but a *favor*...
I'm listening...
CDW 12

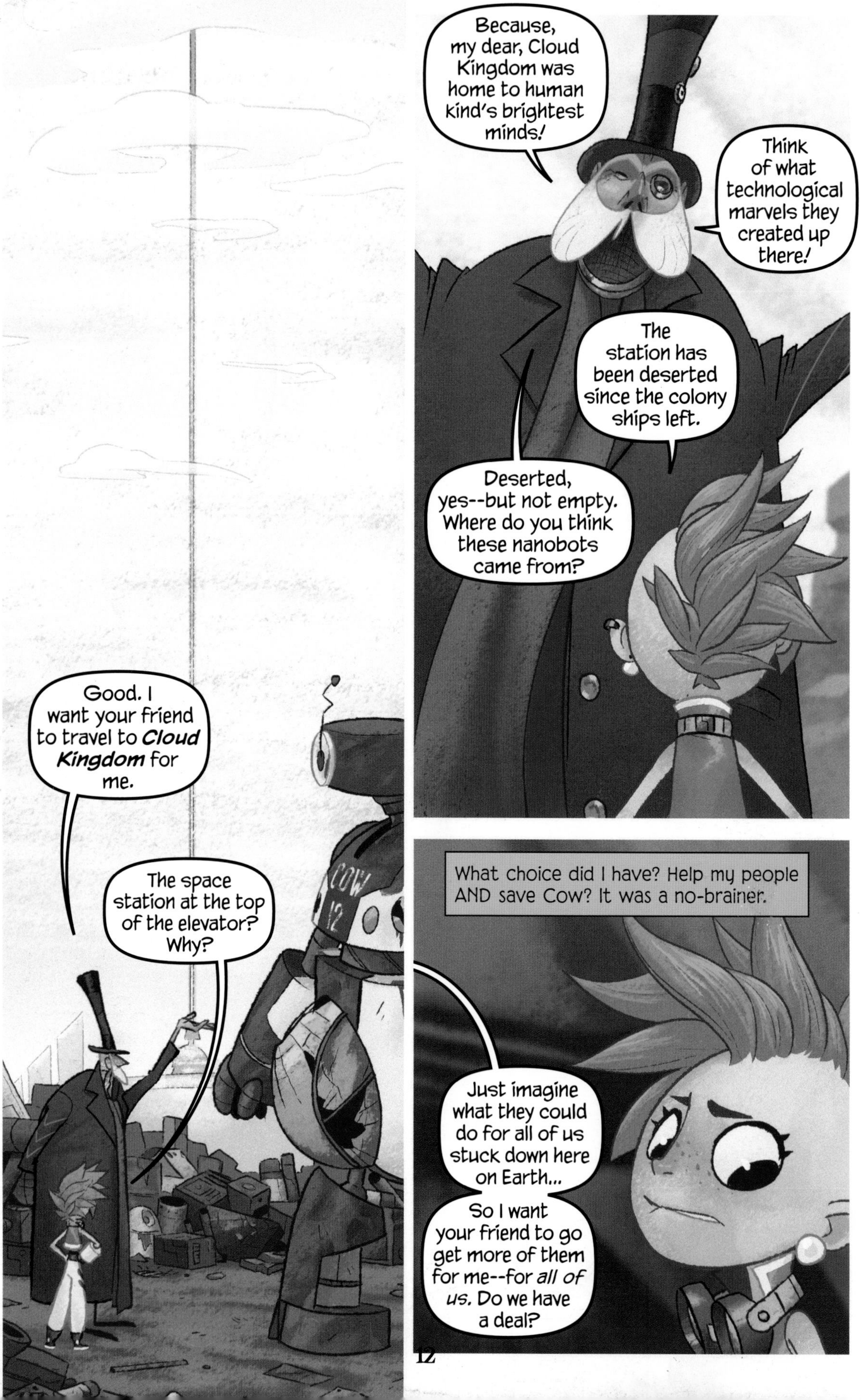
Good. I want your friend to travel to ***Cloud Kingdom*** for me.
The space station at the top of the elevator? Why?
Because, my dear, Cloud Kingdom was home to human kind's brightest minds!
Think of what technological marvels they created up there!
The station has been deserted since the colony ships left.
Deserted, yes--but not empty. Where do you think these nanobots came from?
COW 12
What choice did I have? Help my people AND save Cow? It was a no-brainer.
Just imagine what they could do for all of us stuck down here on Earth...
So I want your friend to go get more of them for me--for *all of us*. Do we have a deal?

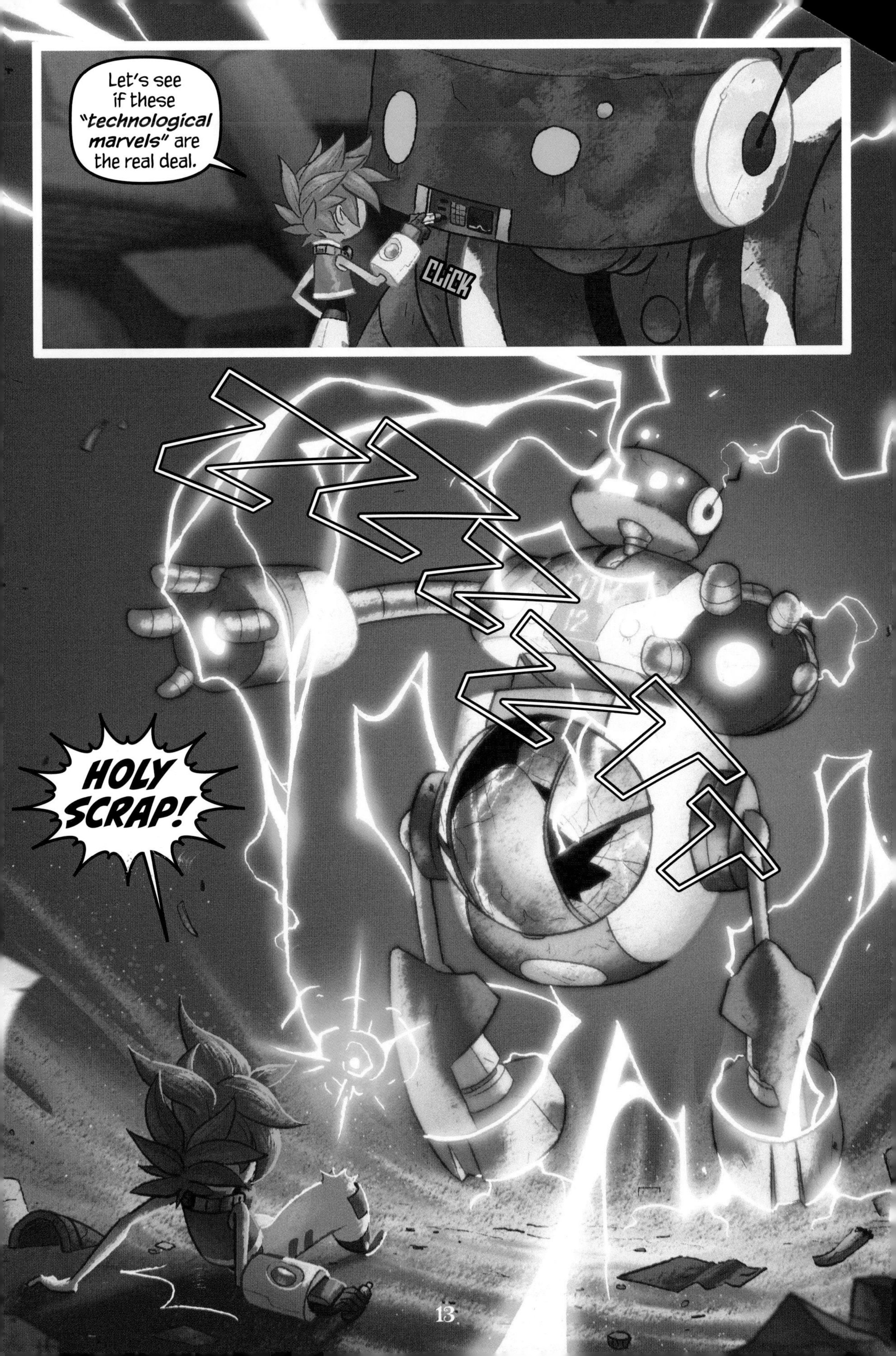

Let's see if these "technological marvels" are the real deal.
CLICK
HOLY SCRAP!

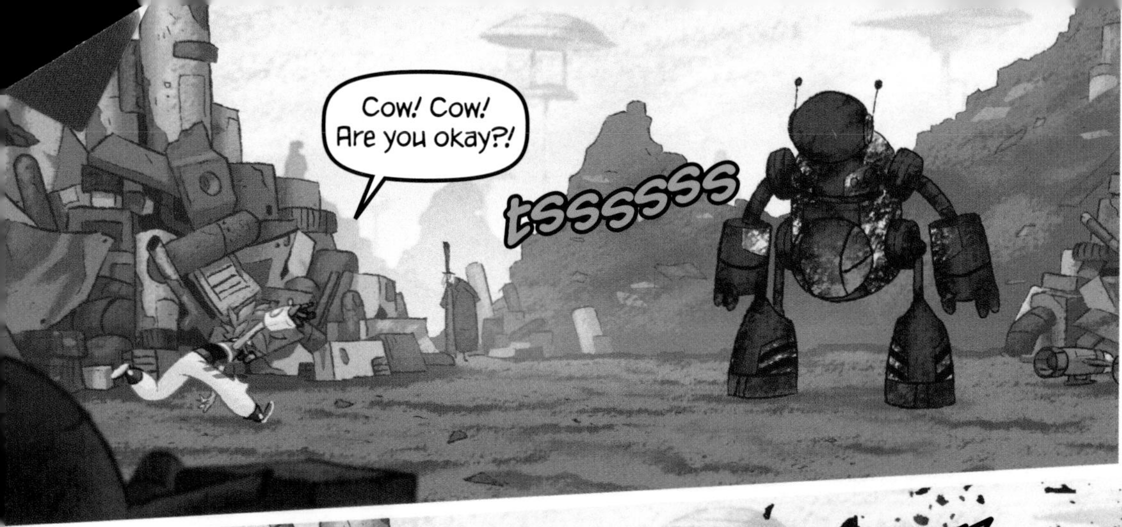
Cow! Cow! Are you okay?!
tssssss

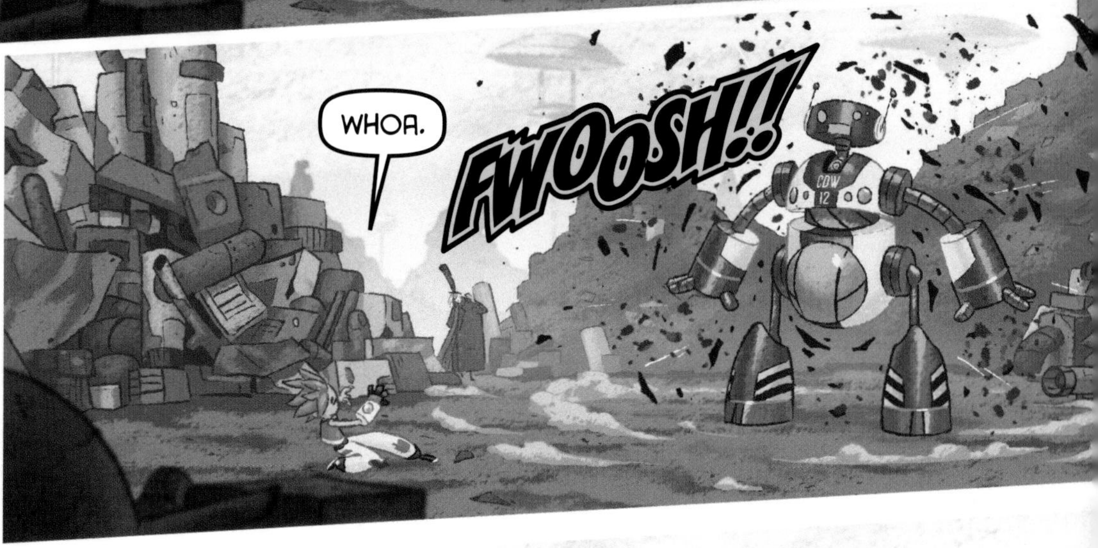
WHOA.
FWOOSH!!
COW 12

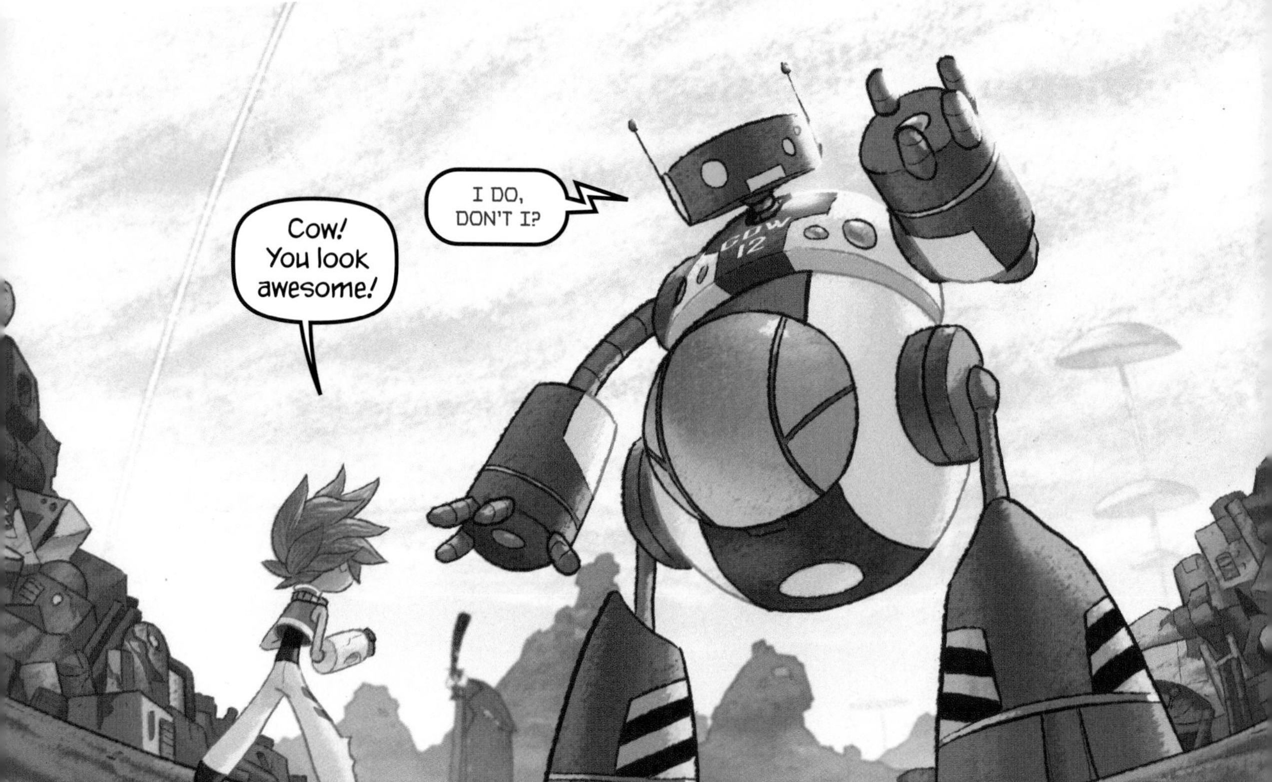
Cow! You look awesome!
I DO, DON'T I?
COW 12

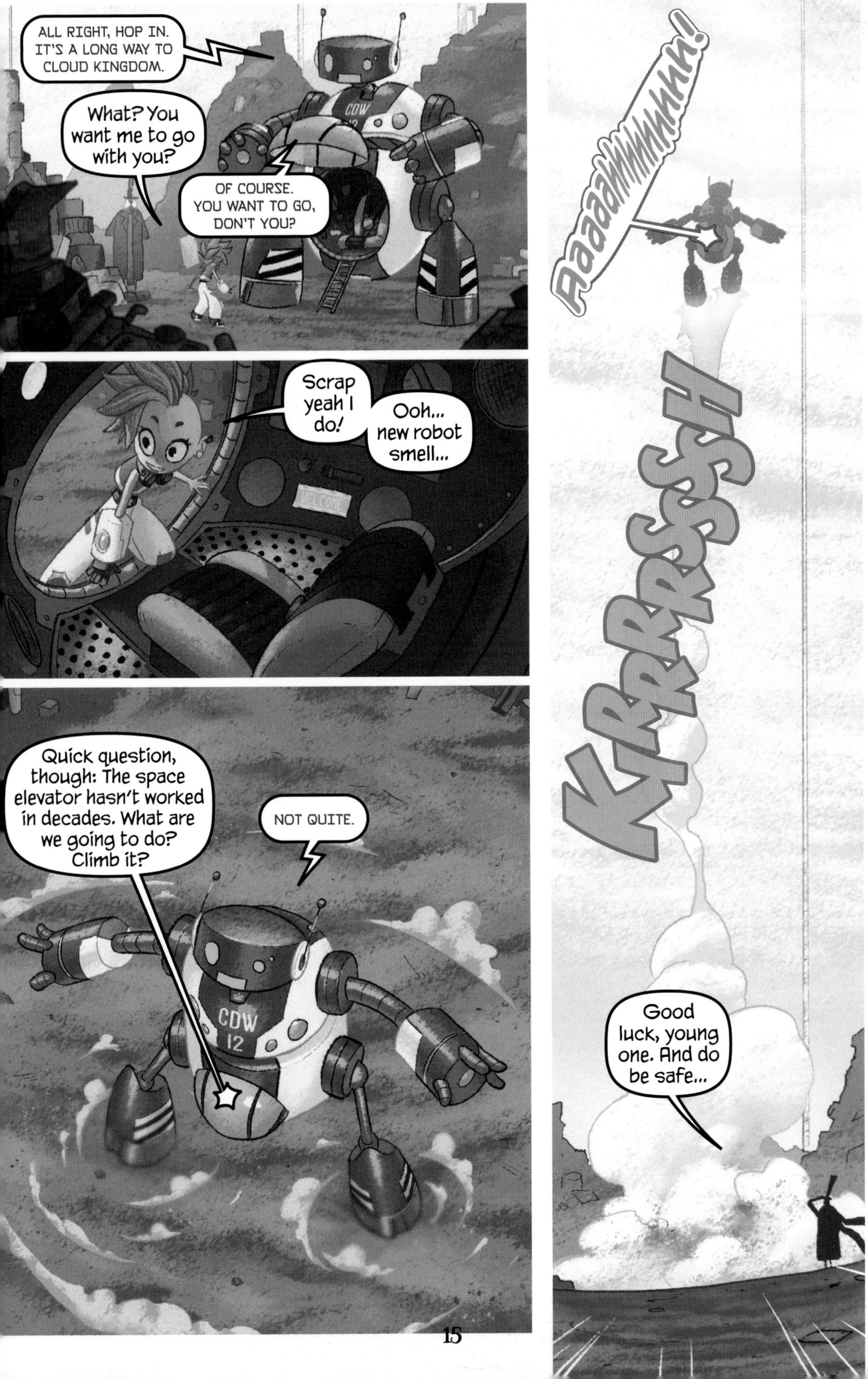
ALL RIGHT, HOP IN. IT'S A LONG WAY TO CLOUD KINGDOM.
What? You want me to go with you?
OF COURSE. YOU WANT TO GO, DON'T YOU?
Scrap yeah I do!
Ooh... new robot smell...
WELCOME
Quick question, though: The space elevator hasn't worked in decades. What are we going to do? Climb it?
NOT QUITE.
CDW 12
Aaaaahhhhhhhh!
KRRRRSSSSH
Good luck, young one. And do be safe...

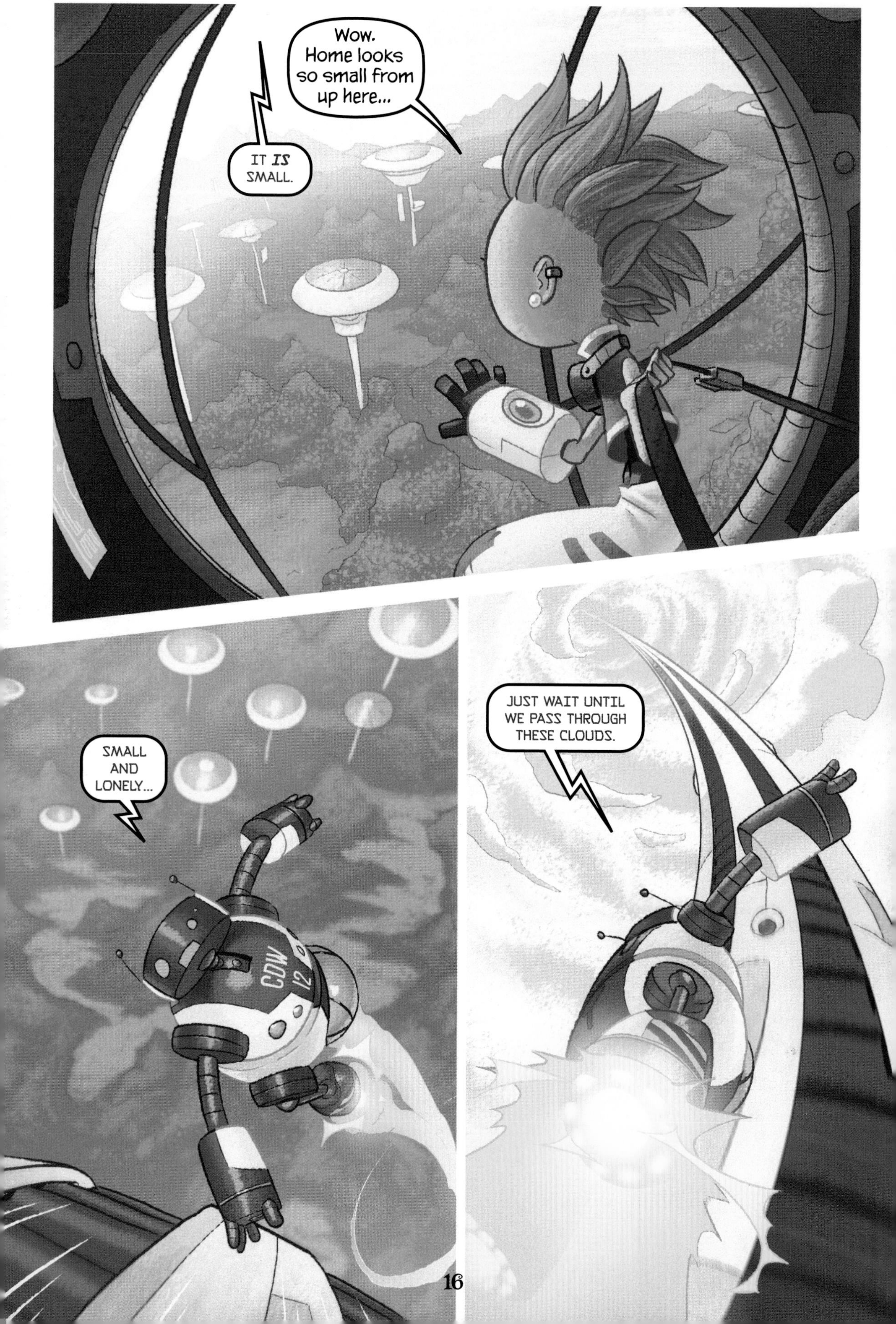
Wow. Home looks so small from up here...
IT IS SMALL.
SMALL AND LONELY...
JUST WAIT UNTIL WE PASS THROUGH THESE CLOUDS.
CDW 12

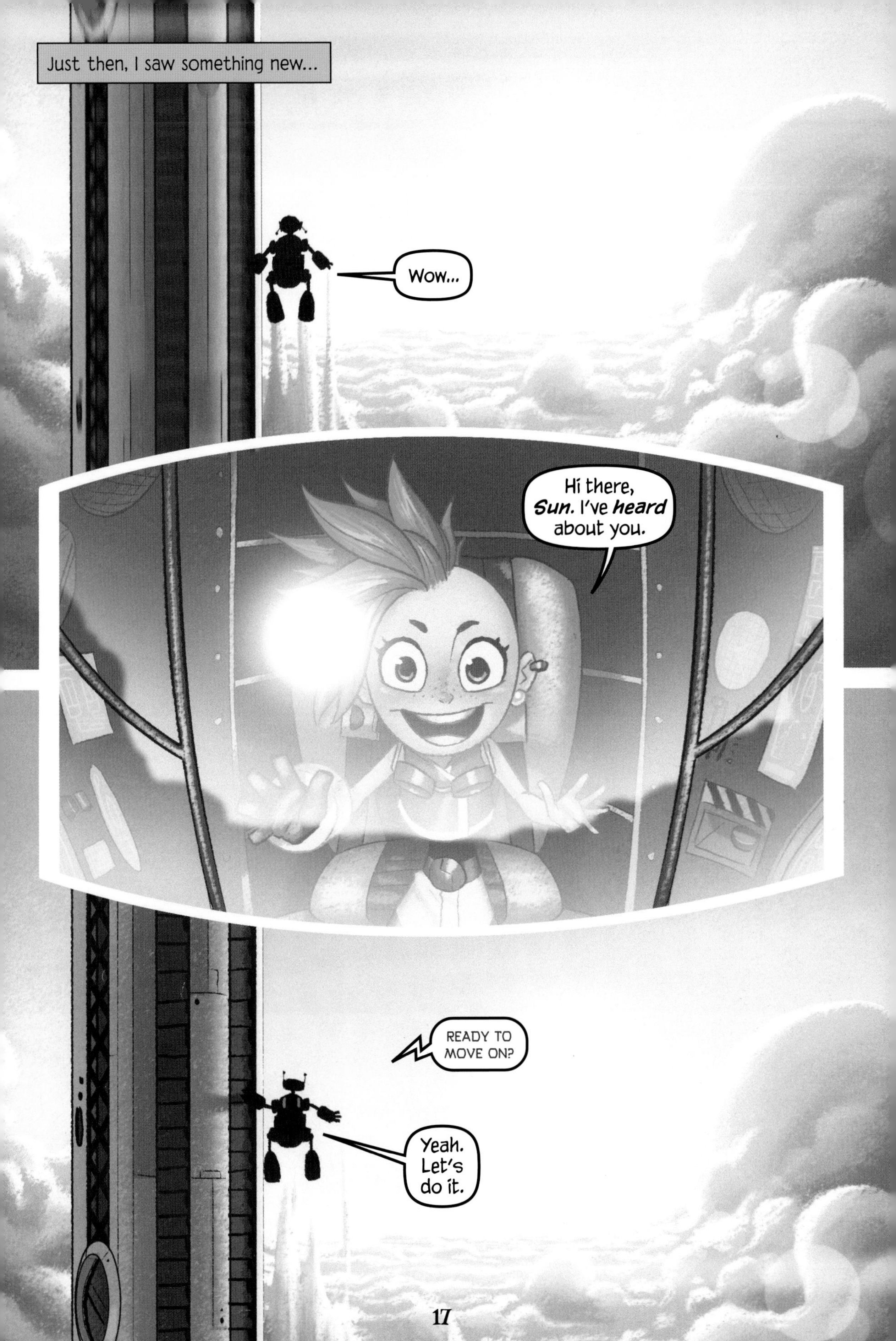
Just then, I saw something new...
Wow...
Hi there, **Sun**. I've **heard** about you.
READY TO MOVE ON?
Yeah. Let's do it.

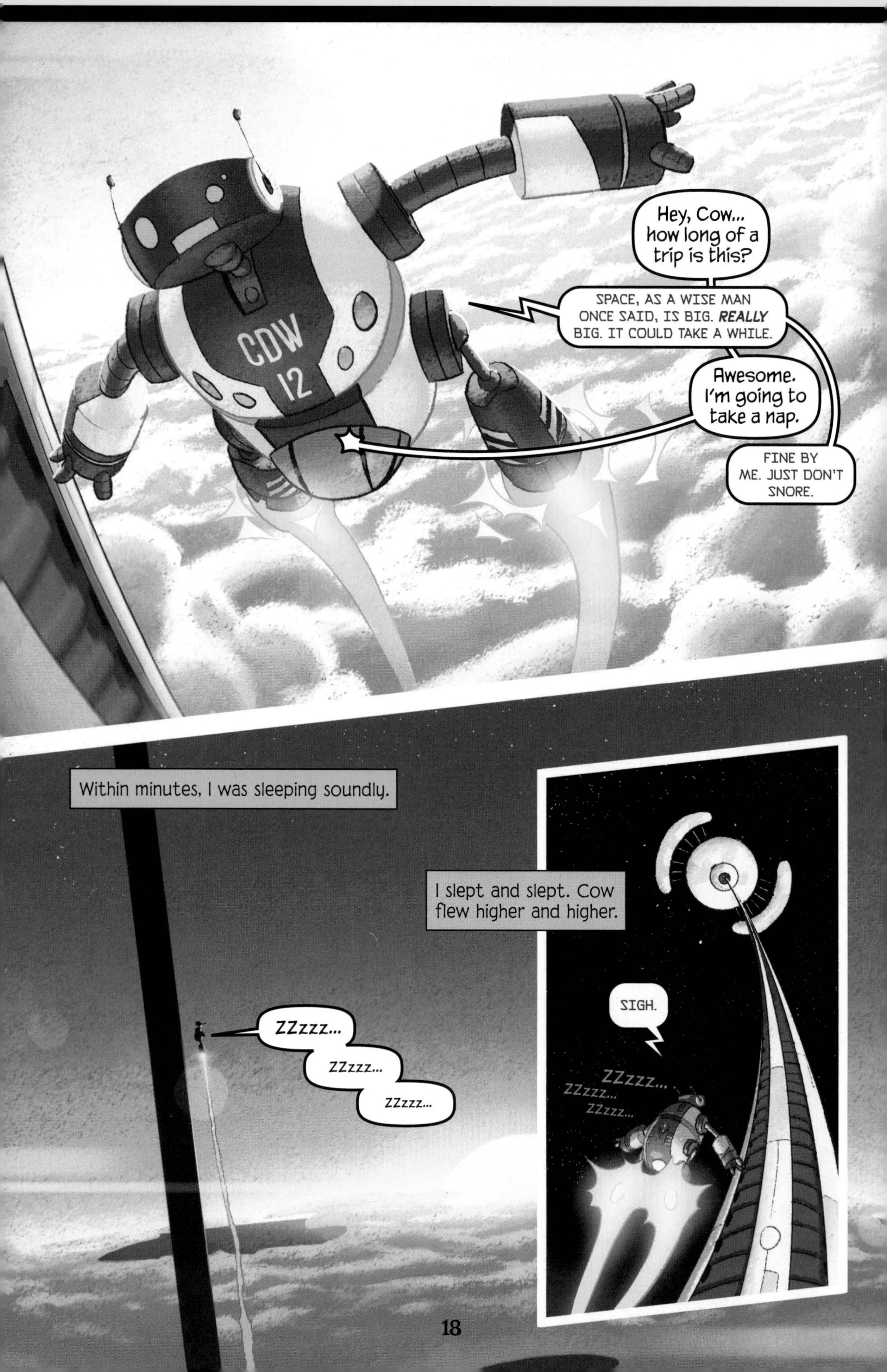
Hey, Cow... how long of a trip is this?
SPACE, AS A WISE MAN ONCE SAID, IS BIG. *REALLY* BIG. IT COULD TAKE A WHILE.
Awesome. I'm going to take a nap.
FINE BY ME. JUST DON'T SNORE.
Within minutes, I was sleeping soundly.
ZZzzz...
ZZzzz...
ZZzzz...
I slept and slept. Cow flew higher and higher.
SIGH.
ZZzzz...
ZZzzz...
ZZzzz...

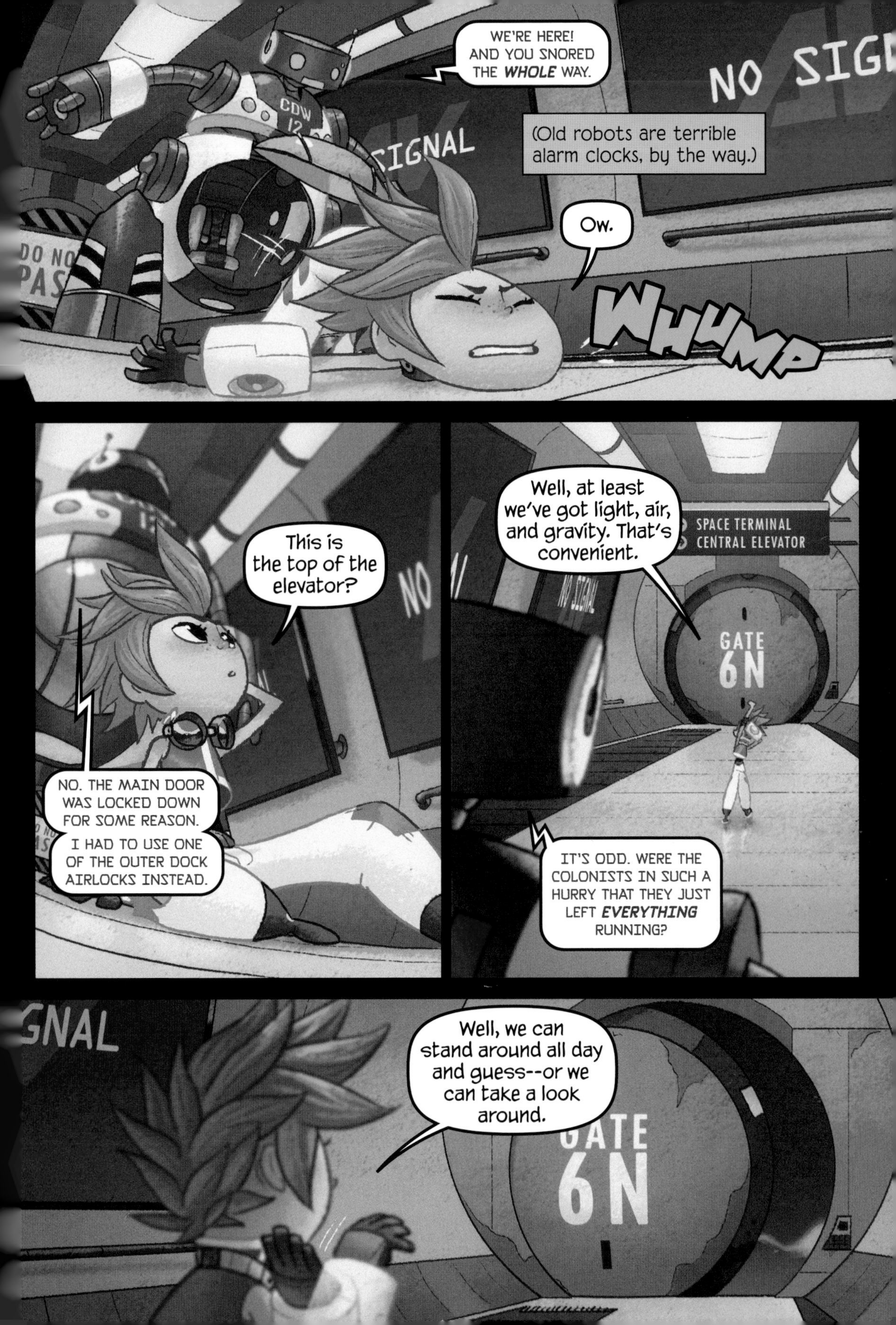

WE'RE HERE! AND YOU SNORED THE ***WHOLE*** WAY.
(Old robots are terrible alarm clocks, by the way.)
Ow.
WHUMP
This is the top of the elevator?
NO. THE MAIN DOOR WAS LOCKED DOWN FOR SOME REASON.
I HAD TO USE ONE OF THE OUTER DOCK AIRLOCKS INSTEAD.
Well, at least we've got light, air, and gravity. That's convenient.
SPACE TERMINAL
CENTRAL ELEVATOR
GATE 6N
IT'S ODD. WERE THE COLONISTS IN SUCH A HURRY THAT THEY JUST LEFT ***EVERYTHING*** RUNNING?
Well, we can stand around all day and guess--or we can take a look around.

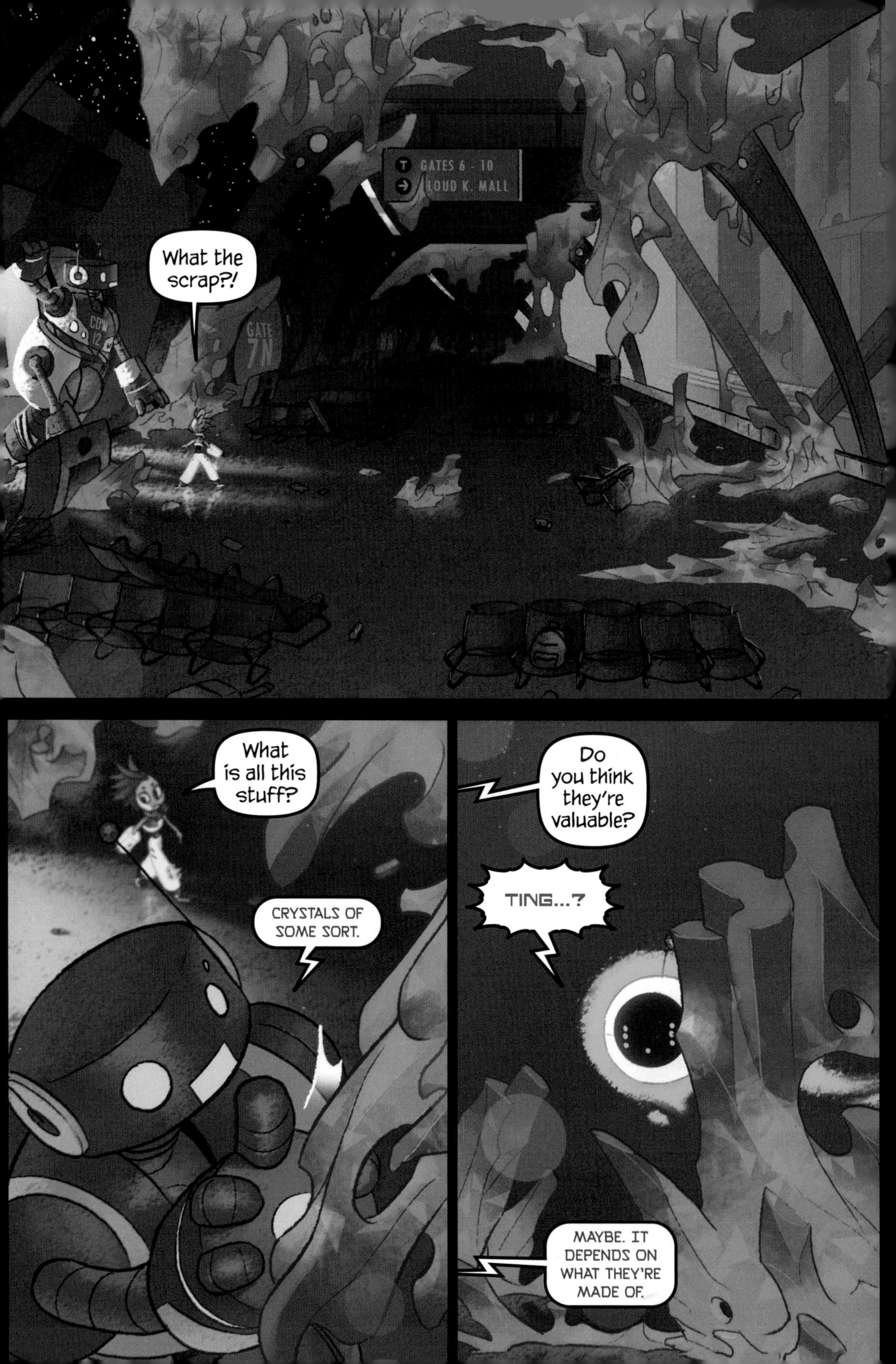
GATES 6 - 10
LOUD K. MALL
GATE 7N
What the scrap?!
What is all this stuff?
CRYSTALS OF SOME SORT.
Do you think they're valuable?
TING...?
MAYBE. IT DEPENDS ON WHAT THEY'RE MADE OF.

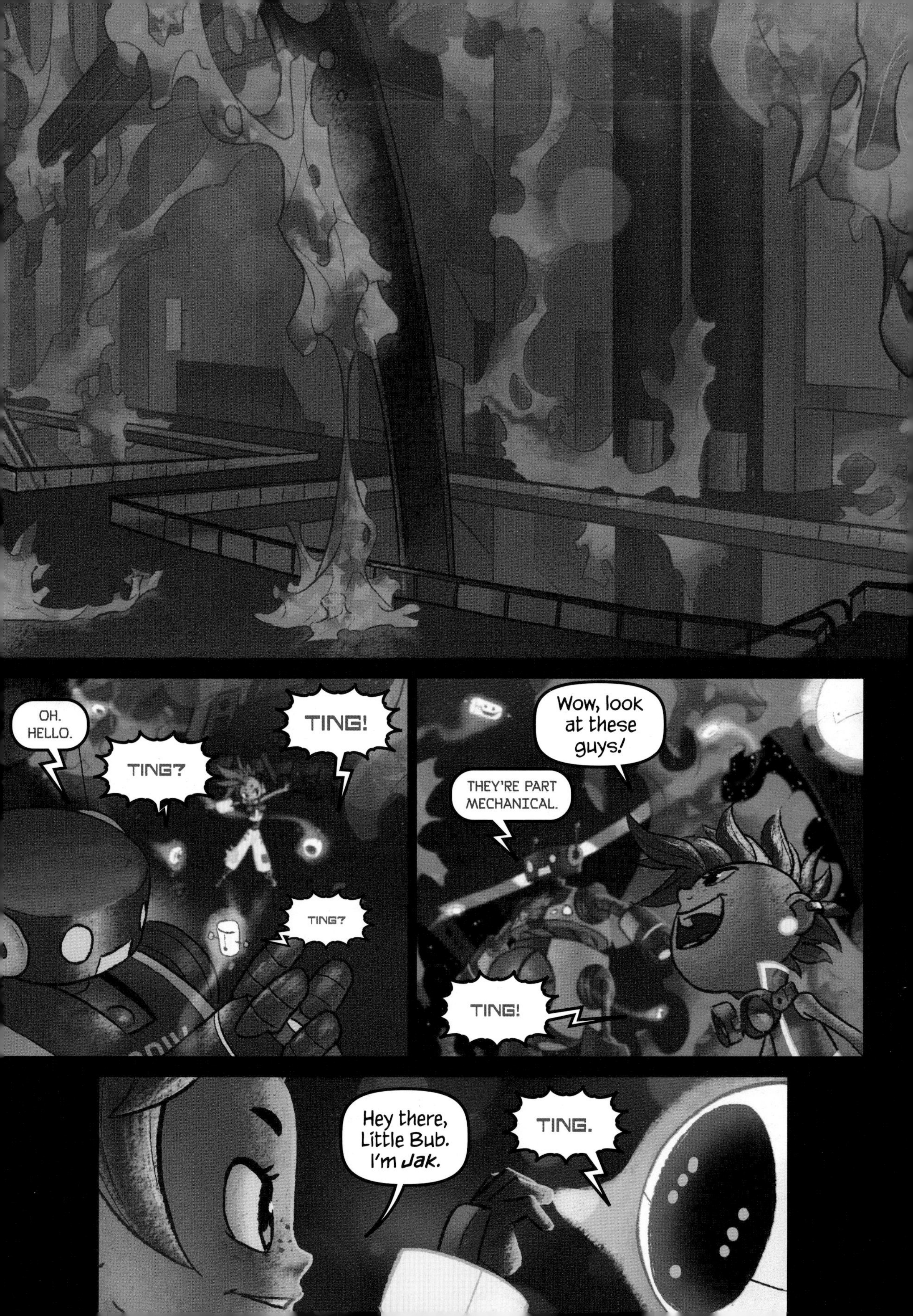
OH. HELLO.
TING?
TING!
TING?
Wow, look at these guys!
THEY'RE PART MECHANICAL.
TING!
Hey there, Little Bub. I'm *Jak*.
TING.

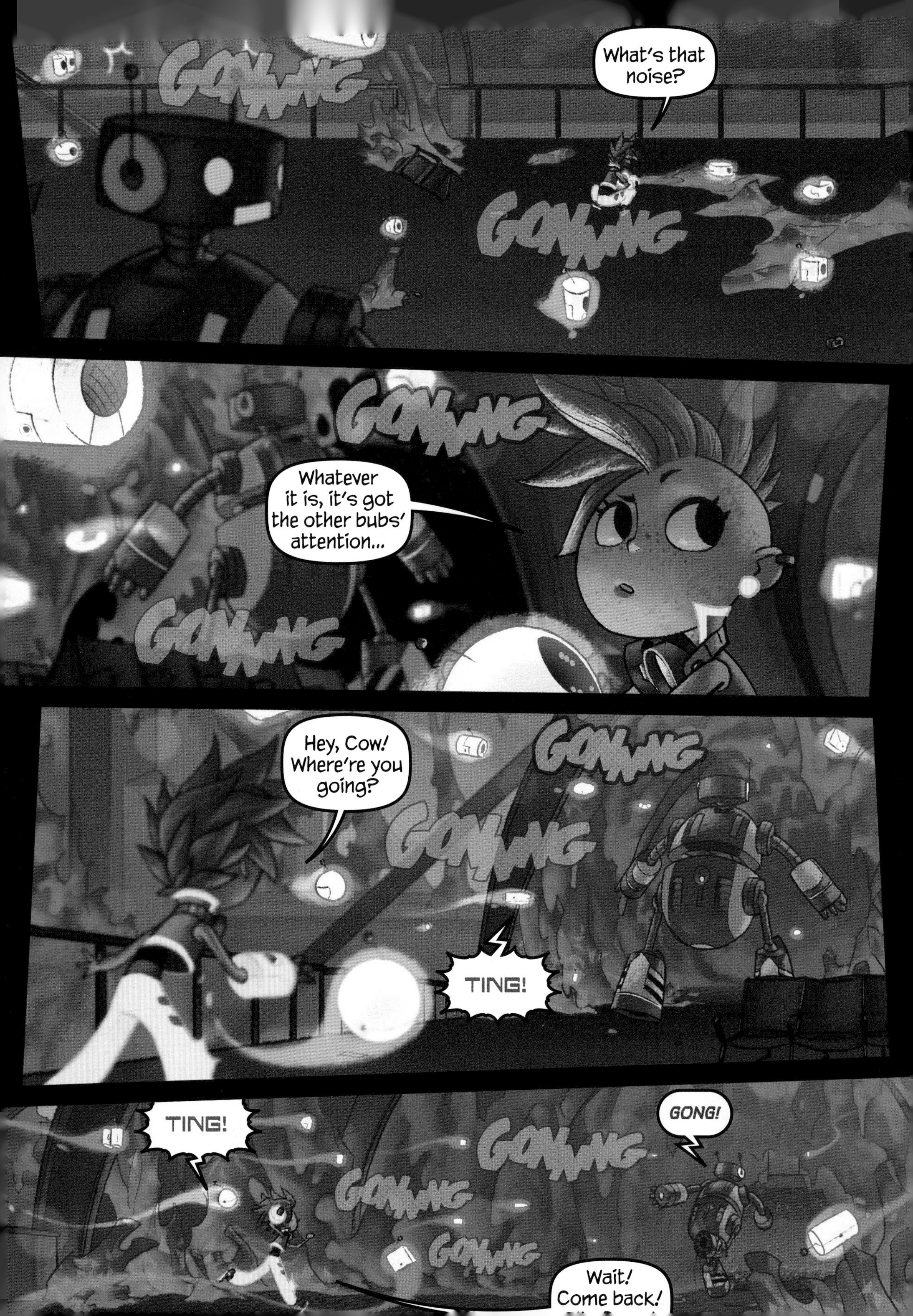
GONNNG
What's that noise?
GONNNG
GONNNG
Whatever it is, it's got the other bubs' attention...
GONNNG
Hey, Cow! Where're you going?
GONNNG
GONNNG
TING!
TING!
GONG!
GONNNG
GONNNG
GONNNG
Wait! Come back!

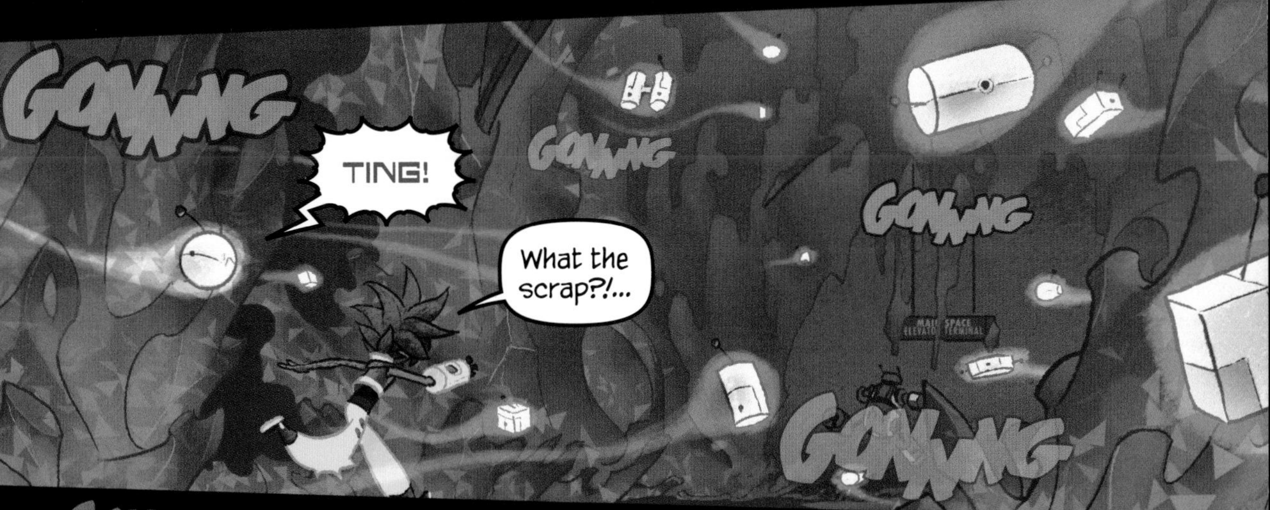
GONNNG
TING!
What the scrap?!...
GONNNG
GONNNG
MAIN SPACE ELEVATOR TERMINAL
GONNNG

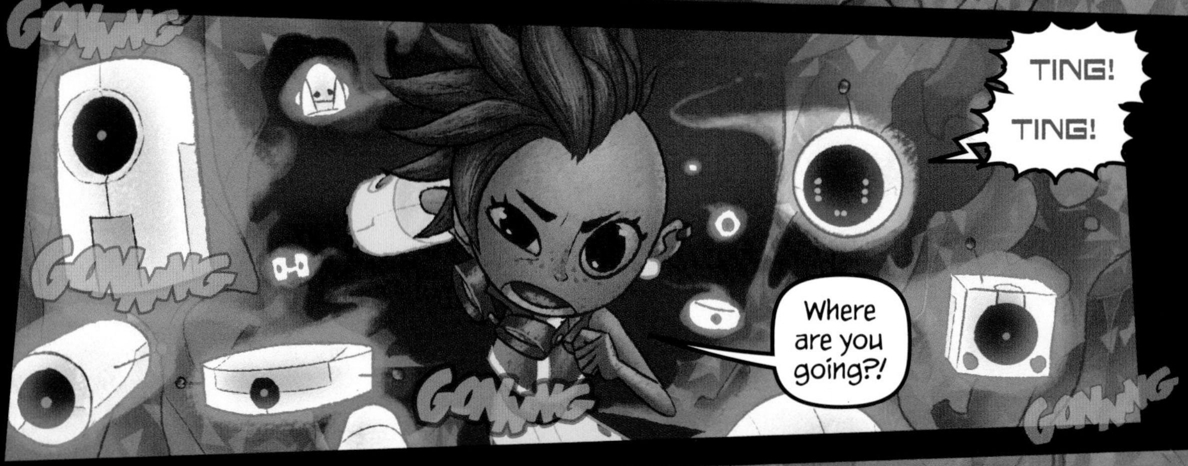
GONNNG
TING!
TING!
GONNNG
Where are you going?!
GONNNG
GONNNG

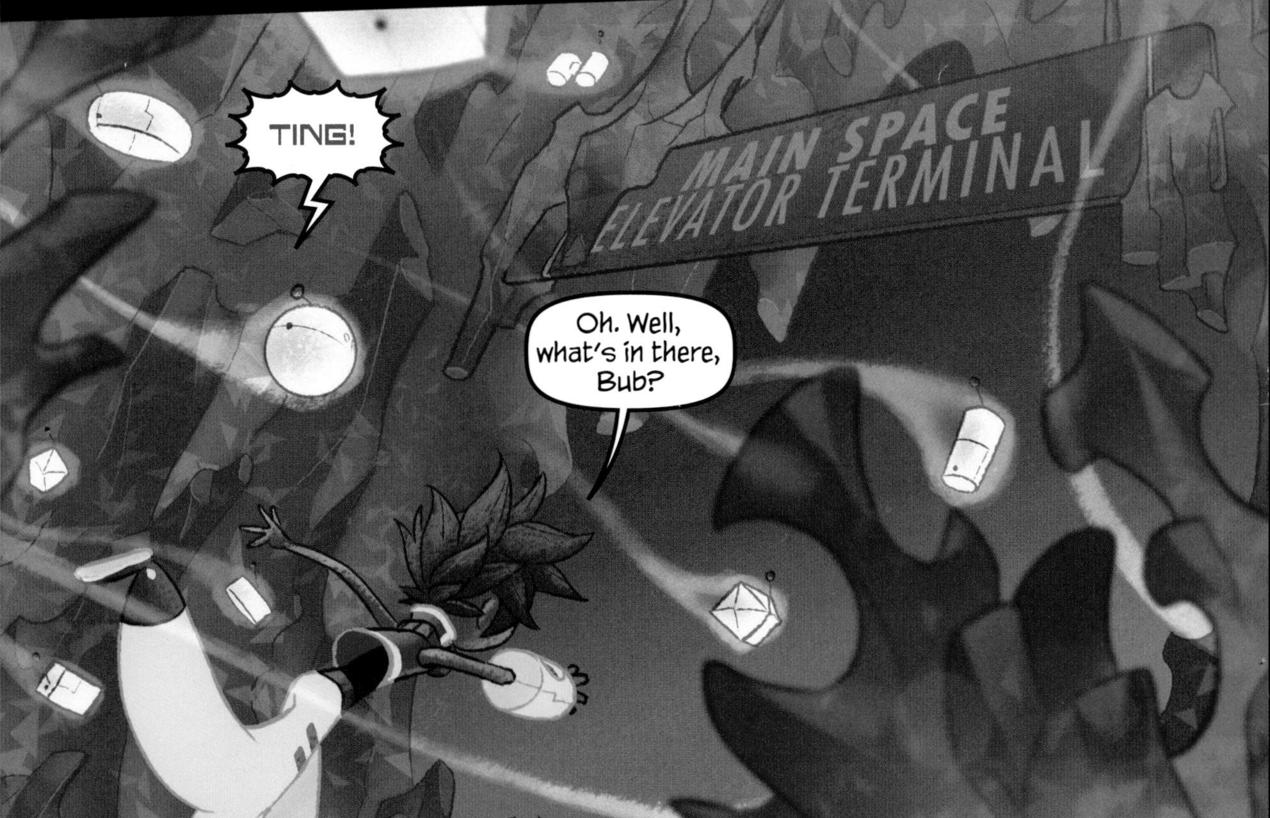
TING!
MAIN SPACE ELEVATOR TERMINAL
Oh. Well, what's in there, Bub?

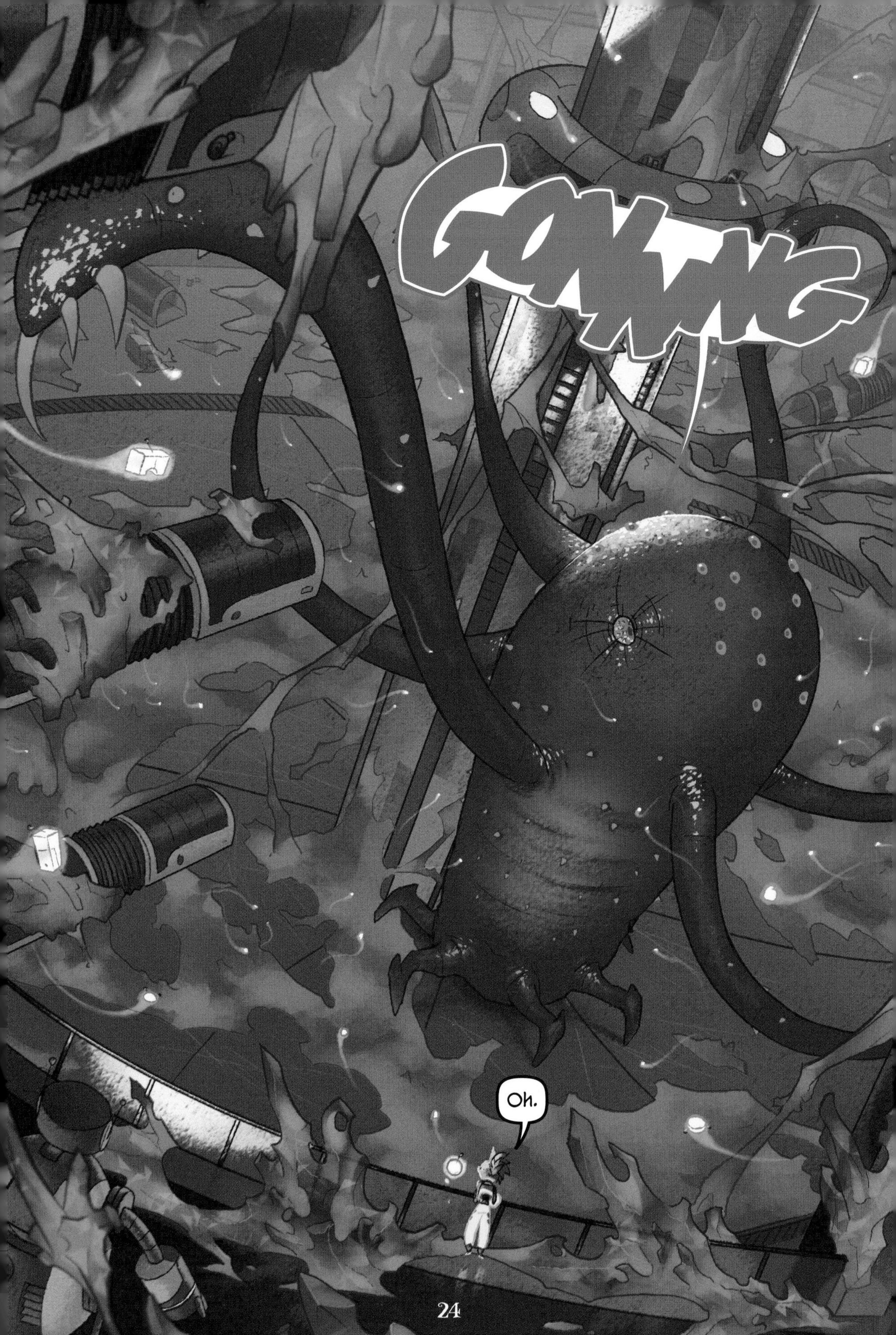
GONNNG
Oh.

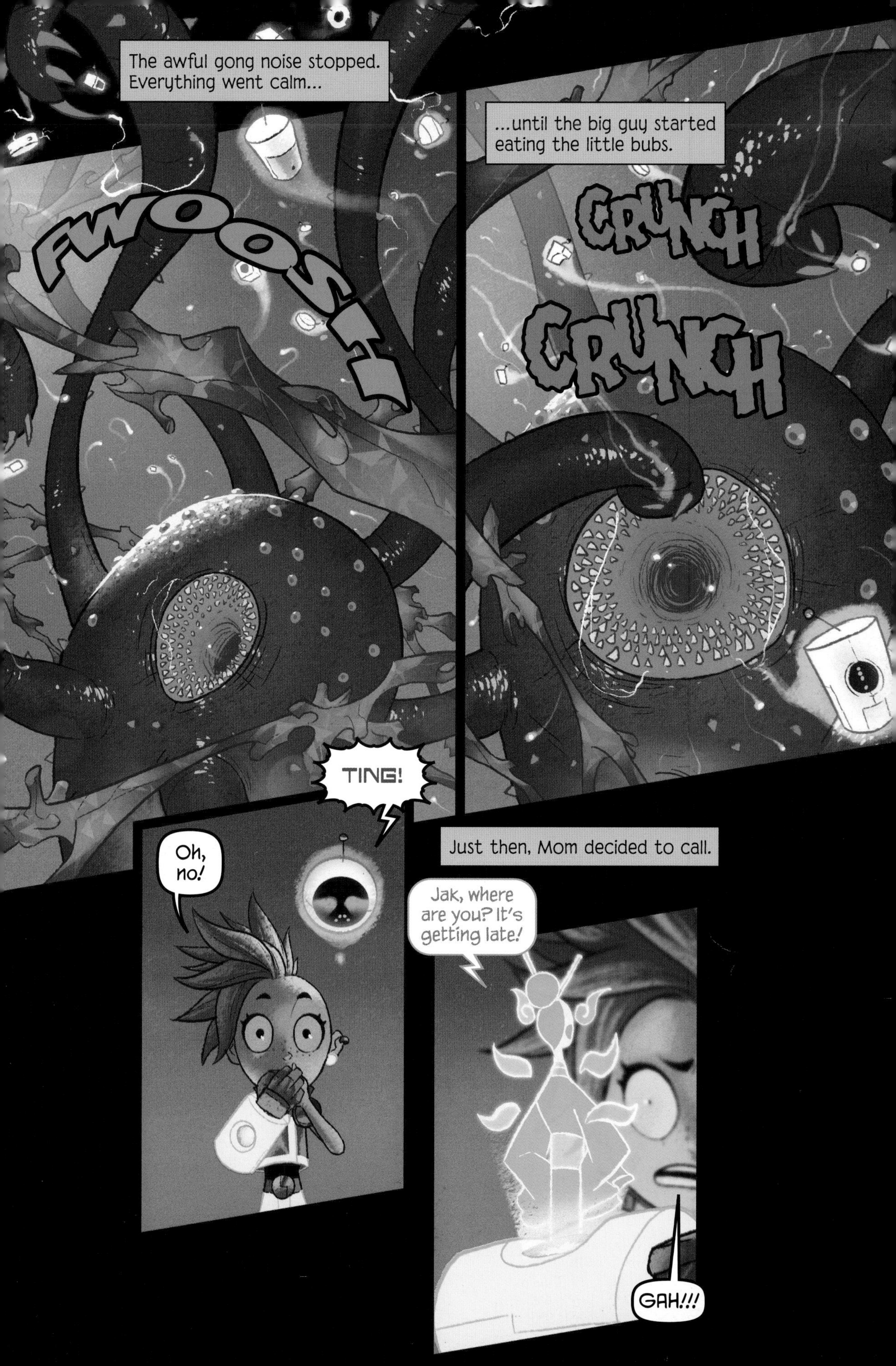

The awful gong noise stopped. Everything went calm...
FWOOSH!
...until the big guy started eating the little bubs.
CRUNCH
CRUNCH
TING!
Oh, no!
Just then, Mom decided to call.
Jak, where are you? It's getting late!
GAH!!!

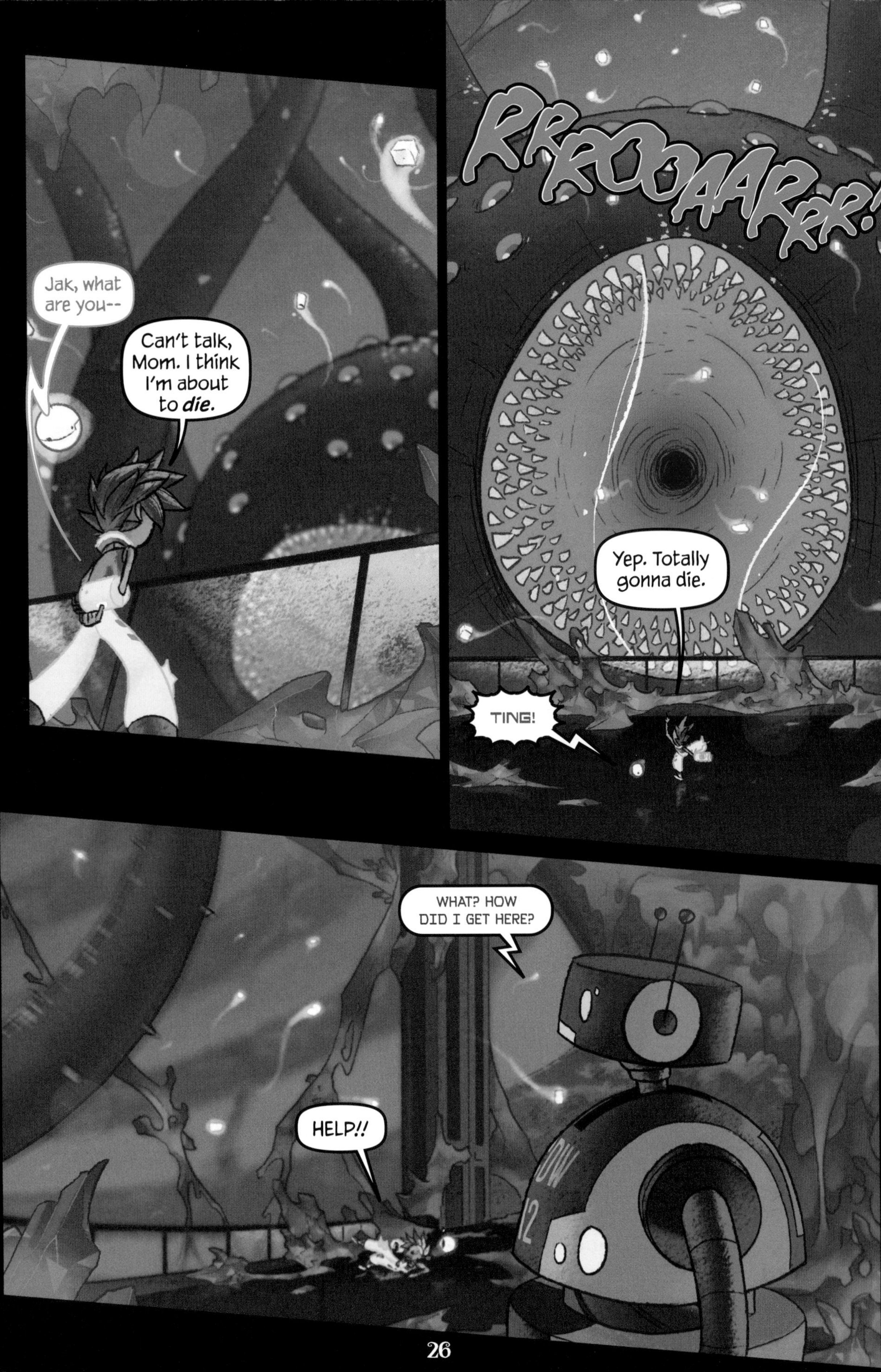
Jak, what are you--
Can't talk, Mom. I think I'm about to *die.*
RRROOAARRR!
Yep. Totally gonna die.
TING!
WHAT? HOW DID I GET HERE?
HELP!!

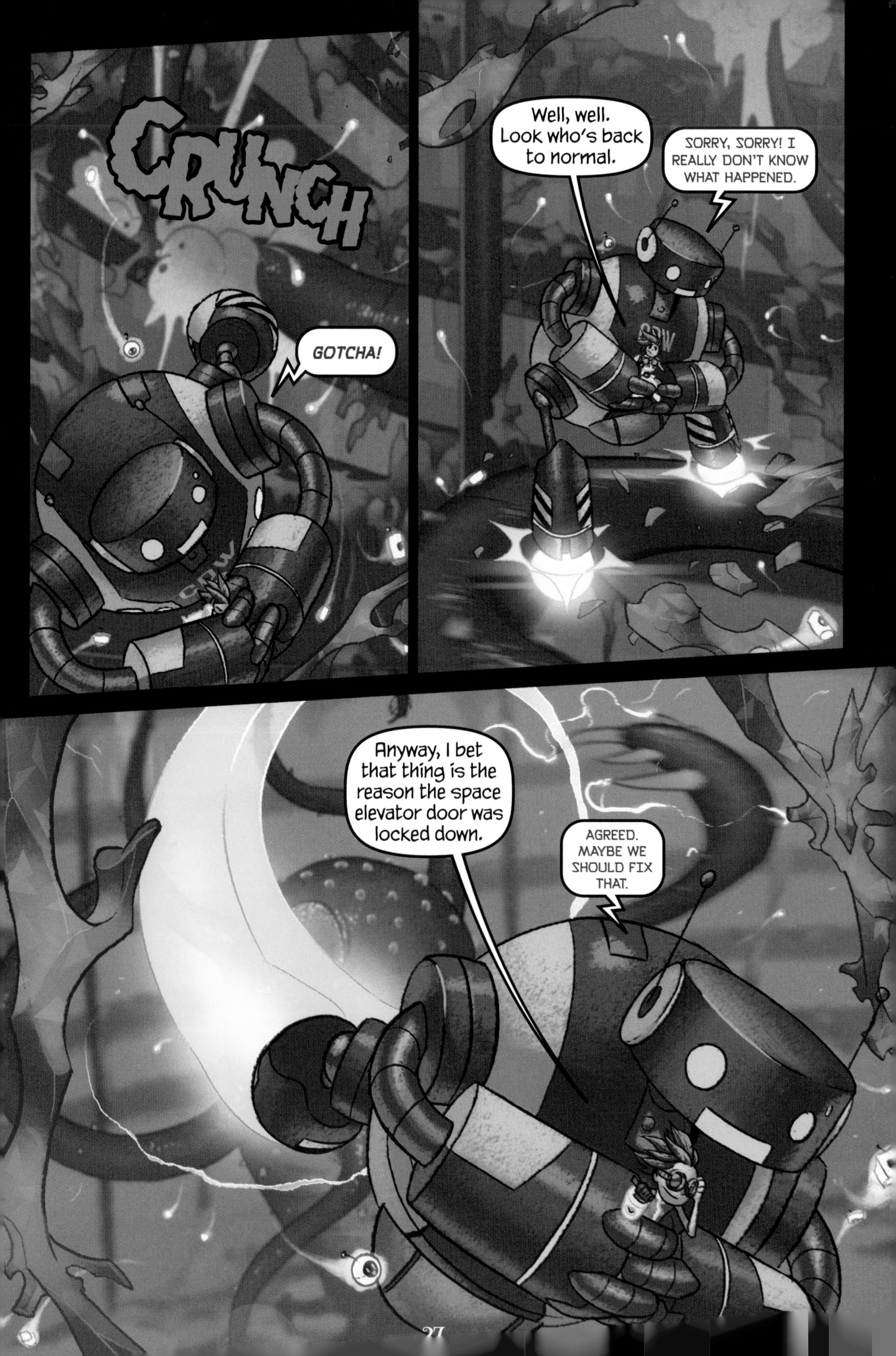
CRUNCH
GOTCHA!
Well, well. Look who's back to normal.
SORRY, SORRY! I REALLY DON'T KNOW WHAT HAPPENED.
Anyway, I bet that thing is the reason the space elevator door was locked down.
AGREED. MAYBE WE SHOULD FIX THAT.

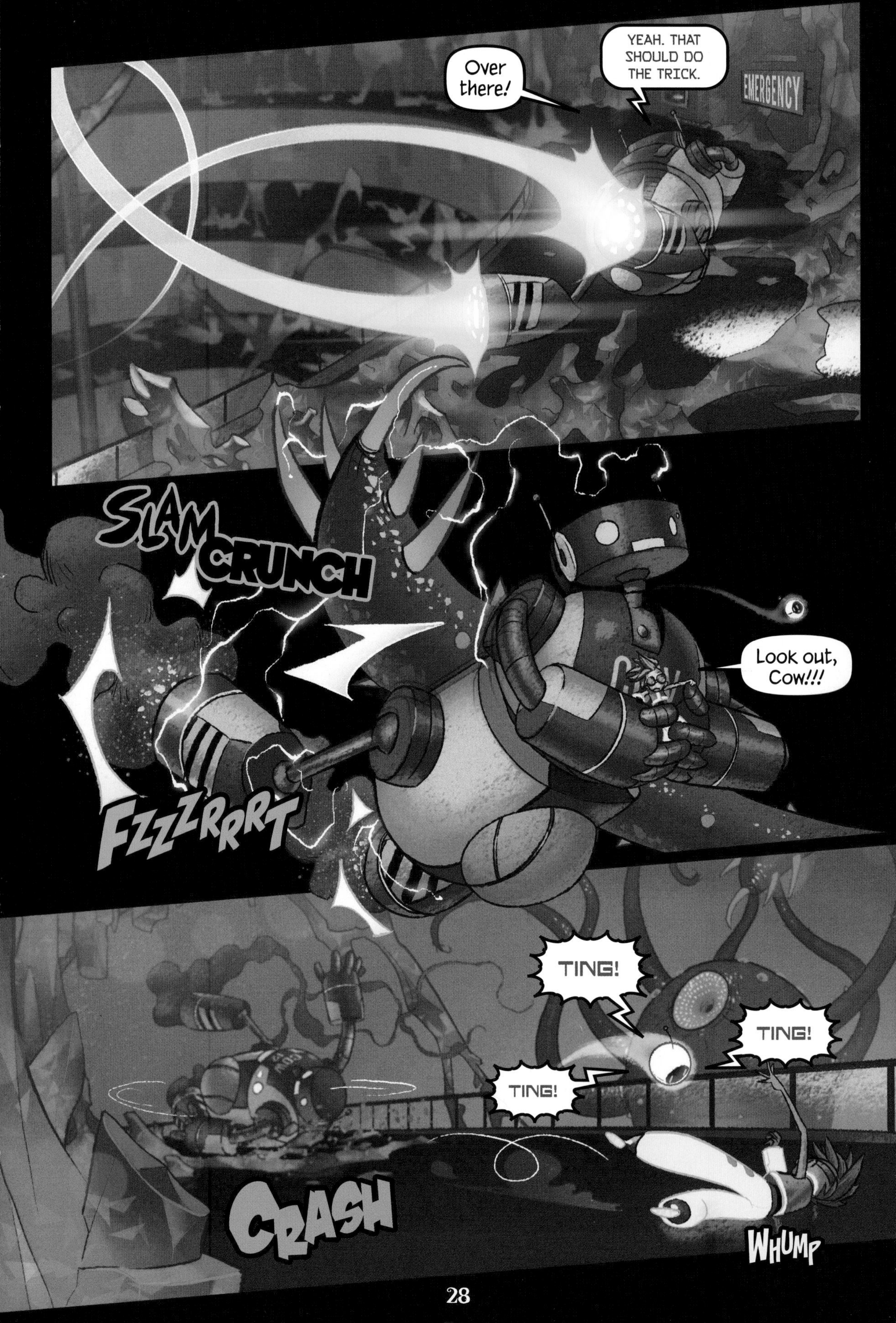

Over there!
YEAH. THAT SHOULD DO THE TRICK.
EMERGENCY
SLAM
CRUNCH
FZZZRRRT
Look out, Cow!!!
TING!
TING!
TING!
CRASH
WHUMP

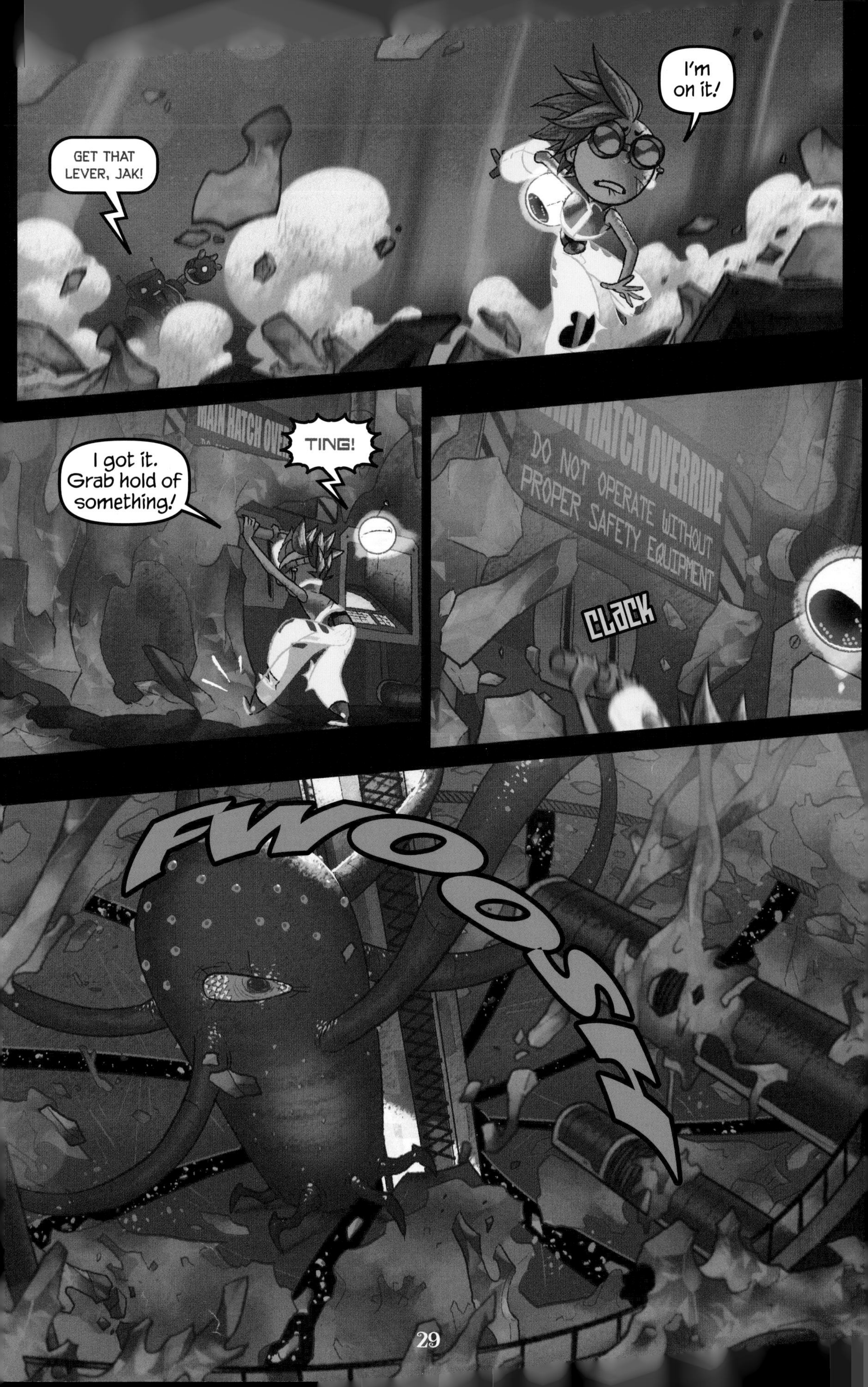
I'm on it!
GET THAT LEVER, JAK!
MAIN HATCH OVE
TING!
I got it. Grab hold of something!
MAIN HATCH OVERRIDE
DO NOT OPERATE WITHOUT PROPER SAFETY EQUIPMENT
CLACK
FWOOSH

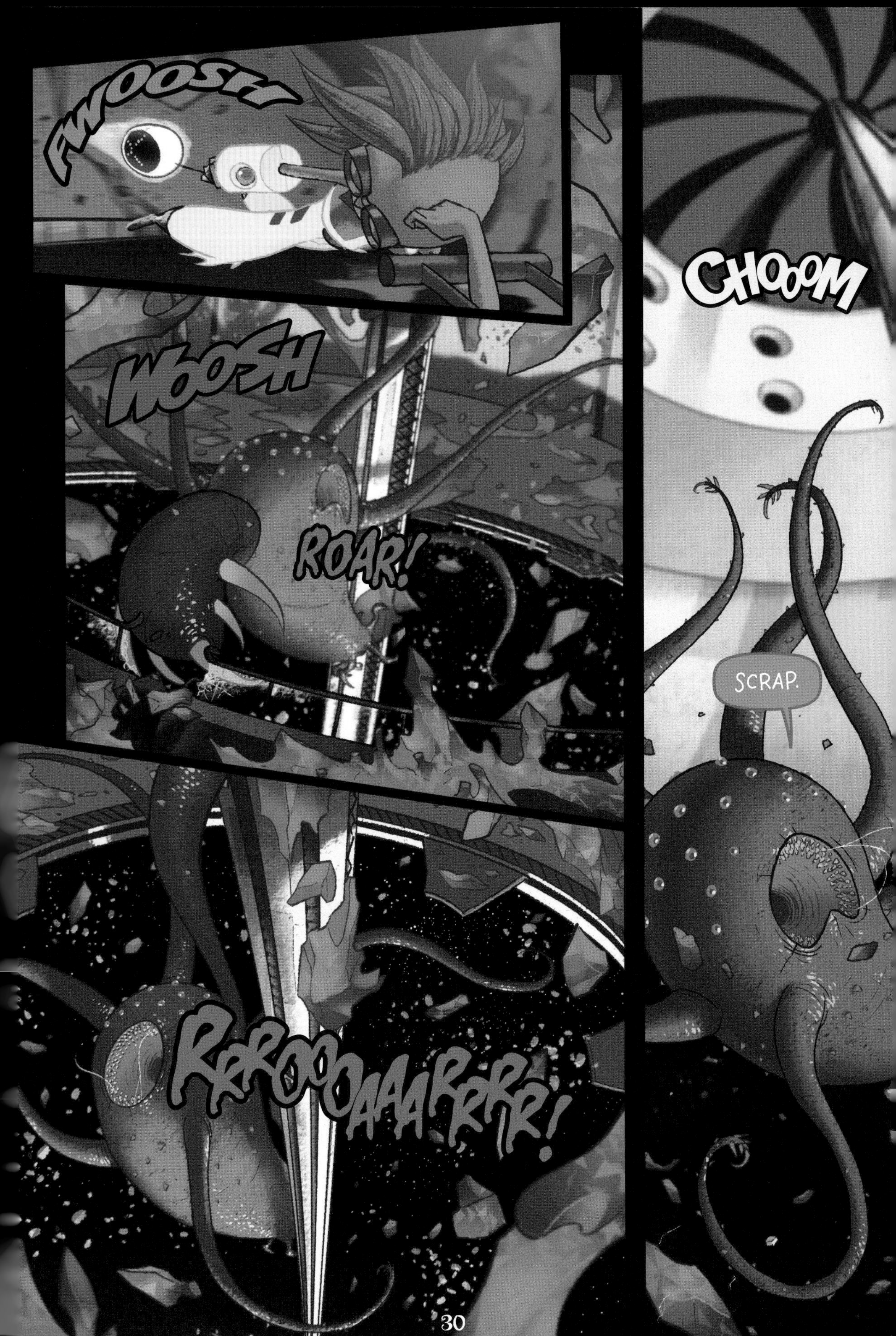
FWOOSH
WOOSH
ROAR!
RRROOOAAARRRR!
CHOOOM
SCRAP.

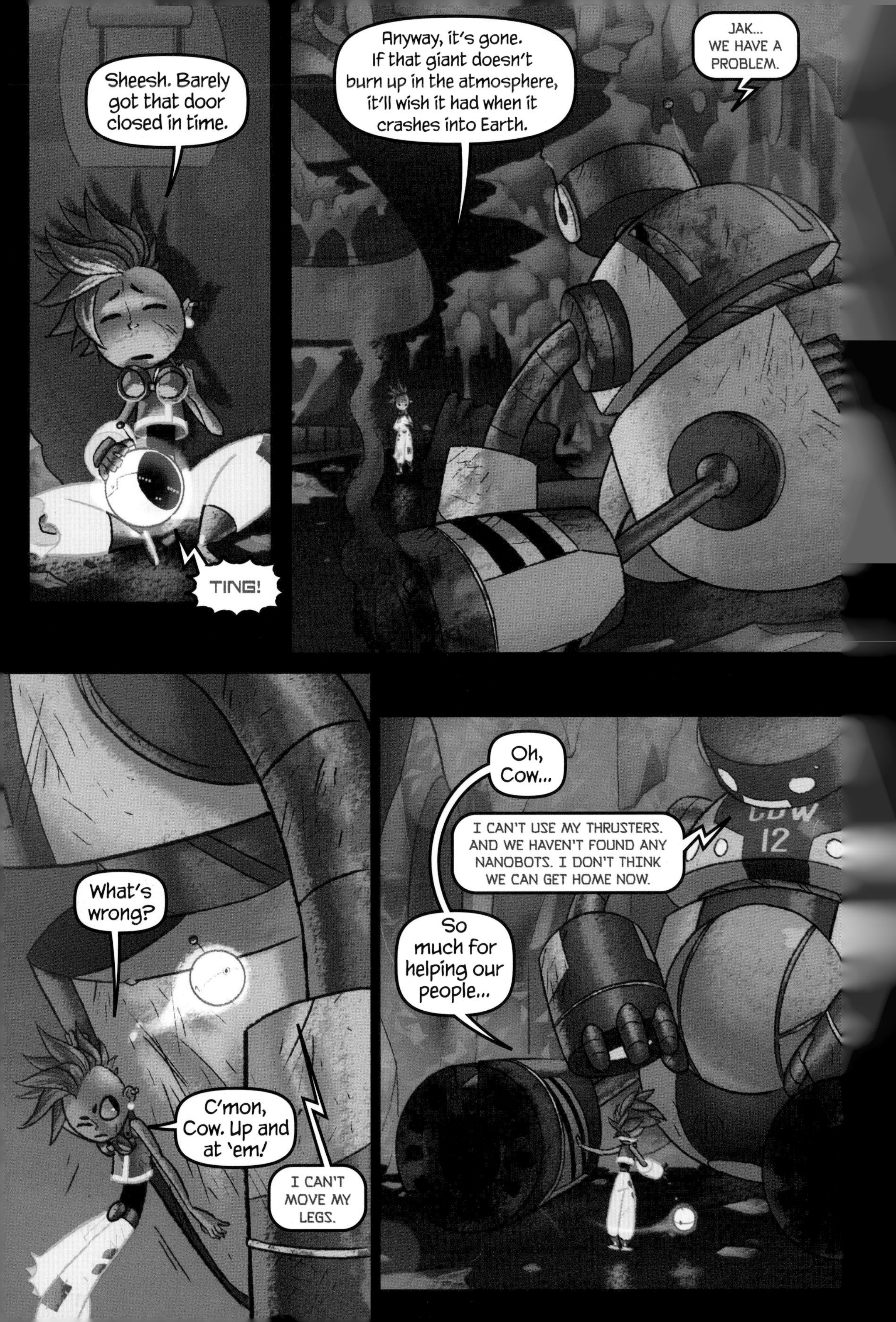
Sheesh. Barely got that door closed in time.
TING!
Anyway, it's gone. If that giant doesn't burn up in the atmosphere, it'll wish it had when it crashes into Earth.
JAK... WE HAVE A PROBLEM.
What's wrong?
C'mon, Cow. Up and at 'em!
I CAN'T MOVE MY LEGS.
Oh, Cow...
I CAN'T USE MY THRUSTERS. AND WE HAVEN'T FOUND ANY NANOBOTS. I DON'T THINK WE CAN GET HOME NOW.
So much for helping our people...
COW
12

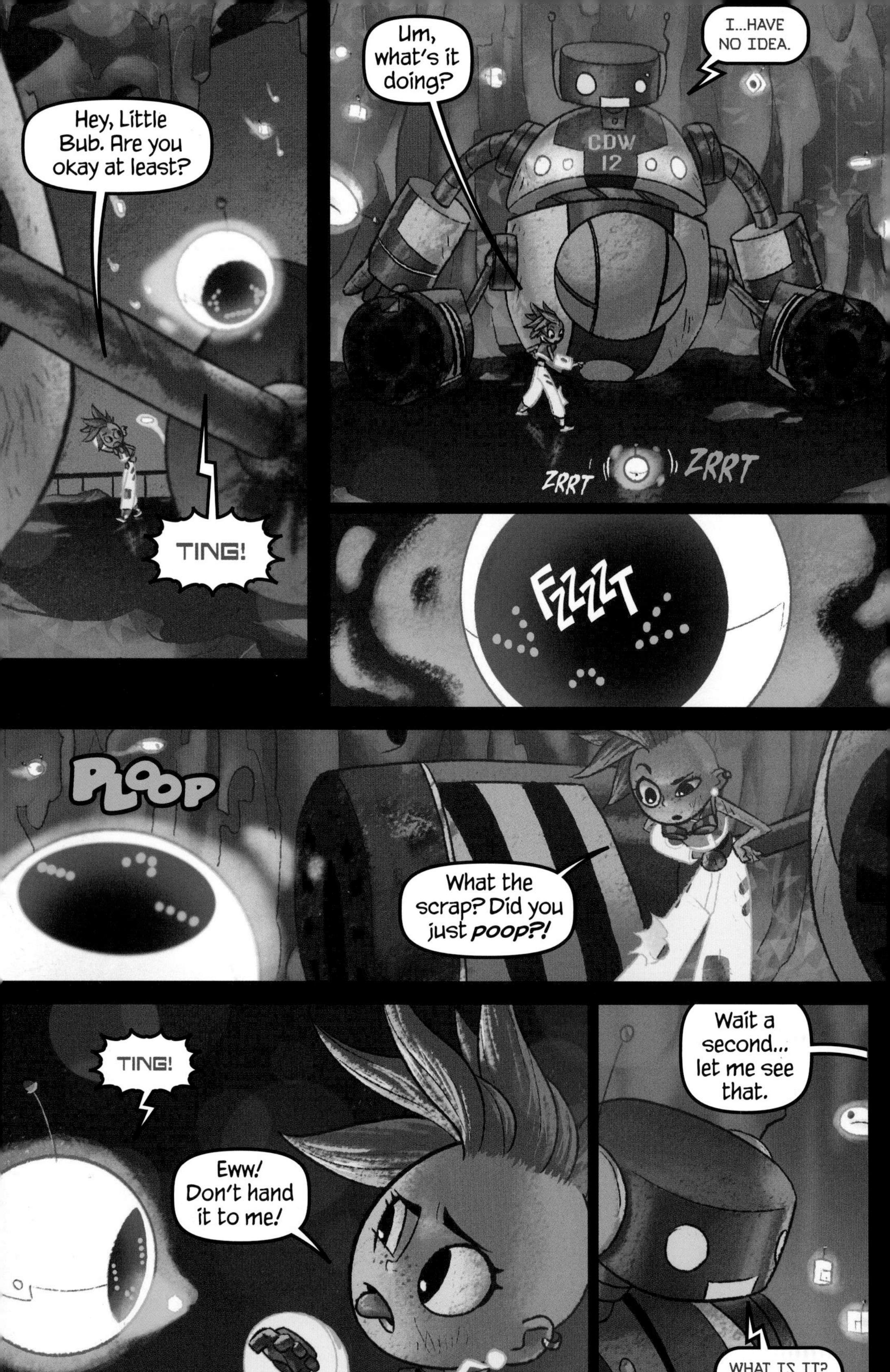
Hey, Little Bub. Are you okay at least?
TING!
Um, what's it doing?
I...HAVE NO IDEA.
ZRRT
ZRRT
FZZZZT
PLOOP
What the scrap? Did you just *poop?!*
TING!
Eww! Don't hand it to me!
Wait a second... let me see that.
WHAT IS IT? IS IT POOP?

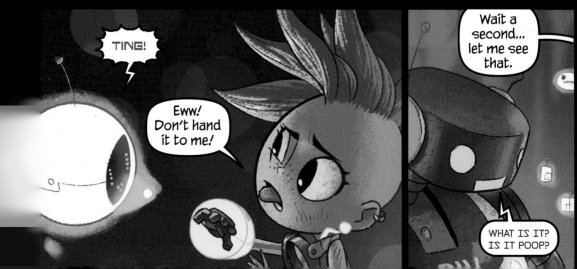

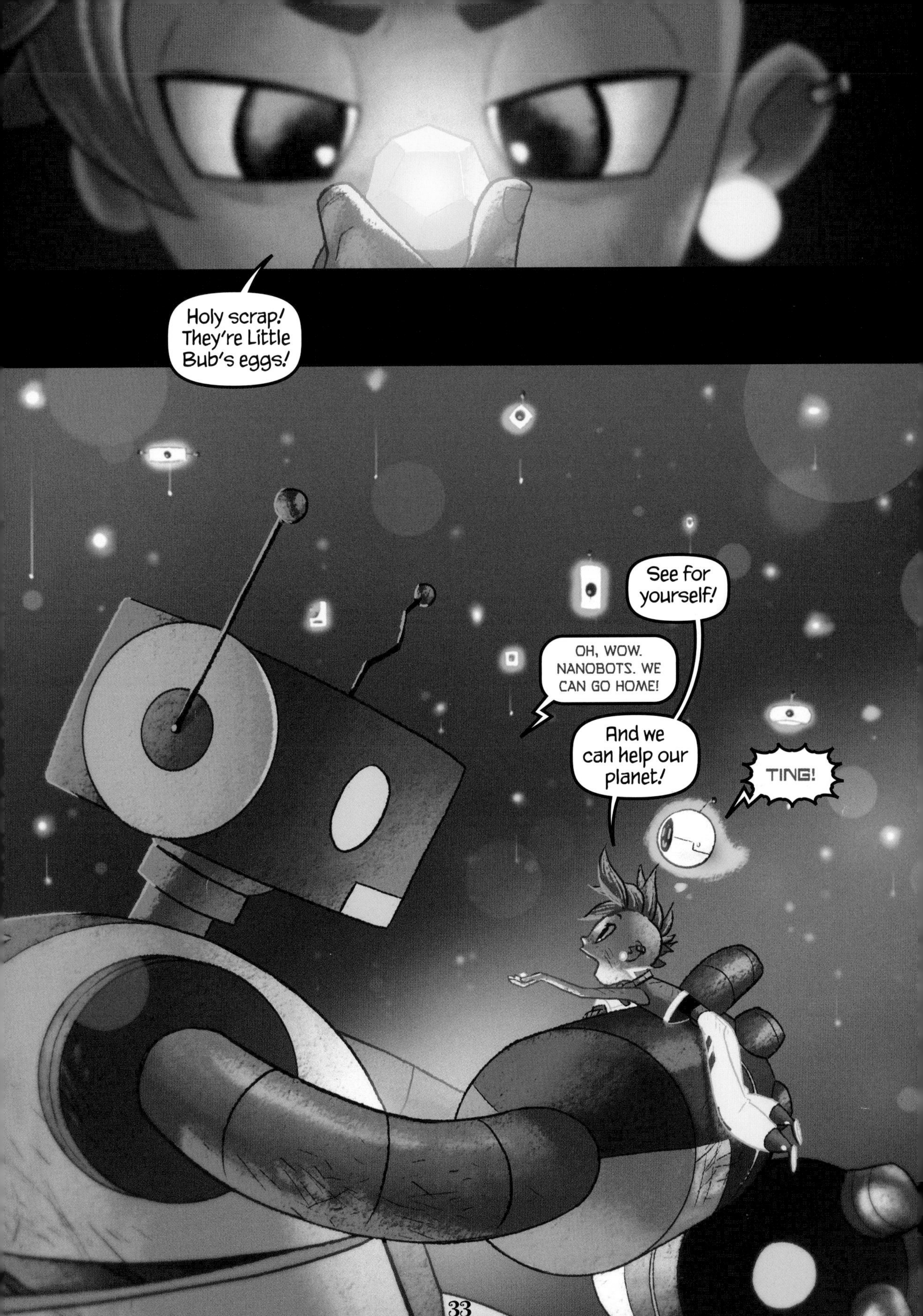
Holy scrap! They're Little Bub's eggs!
See for yourself!
OH, WOW. NANOBOTS. WE CAN GO HOME!
And we can help our planet!
TING!

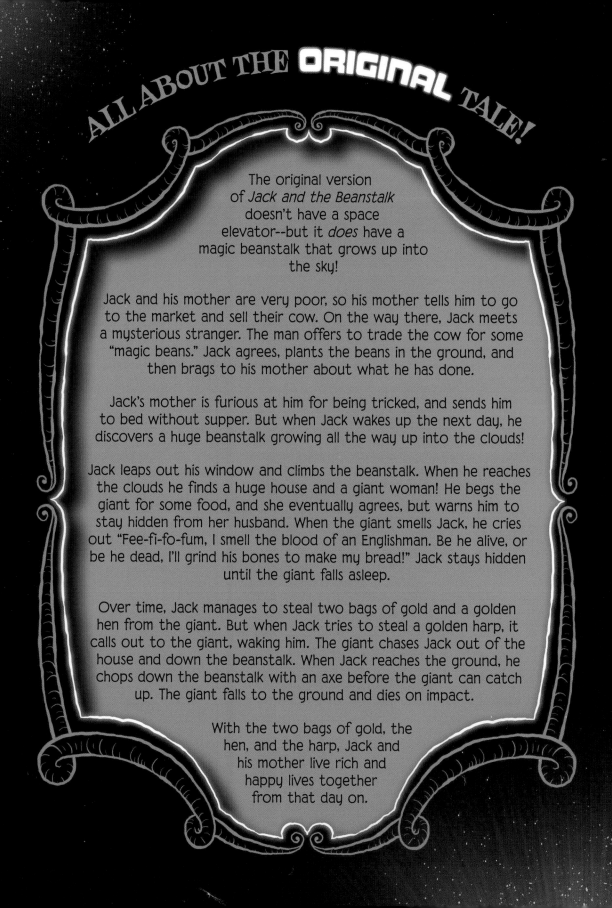

ALL ABOUT THE ORIGINAL TALE!

The original version
of *Jack and the Beanstalk*
doesn't have a space
elevator--but it *does* have a
magic beanstalk that grows up into
the sky!

Jack and his mother are very poor, so his mother tells him to go
to the market and sell their cow. On the way there, Jack meets
a mysterious stranger. The man offers to trade the cow for some
"magic beans." Jack agrees, plants the beans in the ground, and
then brags to his mother about what he has done.

Jack's mother is furious at him for being tricked, and sends him
to bed without supper. But when Jack wakes up the next day, he
discovers a huge beanstalk growing all the way up into the clouds!

Jack leaps out his window and climbs the beanstalk. When he reaches
the clouds he finds a huge house and a giant woman! He begs the
giant for some food, and she eventually agrees, but warns him to
stay hidden from her husband. When the giant smells Jack, he cries
out "Fee-fi-fo-fum, I smell the blood of an Englishman. Be he alive, or
be he dead, I'll grind his bones to make my bread!" Jack stays hidden
until the giant falls asleep.

Over time, Jack manages to steal two bags of gold and a golden
hen from the giant. But when Jack tries to steal a golden harp, it
calls out to the giant, waking him. The giant chases Jack out of the
house and down the beanstalk. When Jack reaches the ground, he
chops down the beanstalk with an axe before the giant can catch
up. The giant falls to the ground and dies on impact.

With the two bags of gold, the
hen, and the harp, Jack and
his mother live rich and
happy lives together
from that day on.

A FAR OUT GUIDE TO THE TALE'S SCI-FI TWISTS!

In the original story, Jack is a young boy. In this version, "Jak" is a young girl!

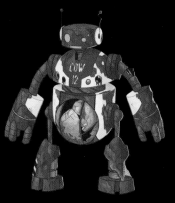

Milky-white, the cow from the fairy tale, is replaced by CDW-12, a robot named Cow.

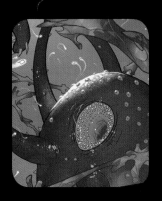

While a giant man tried to eat Jack in the fairy tale, Jak gets attacked by an octopus-like space monster!

And the magic beans from the original tale have become tiny robots that fix up Jak's robotic pal, CDW-12!

VISUAL QUESTIONS

1

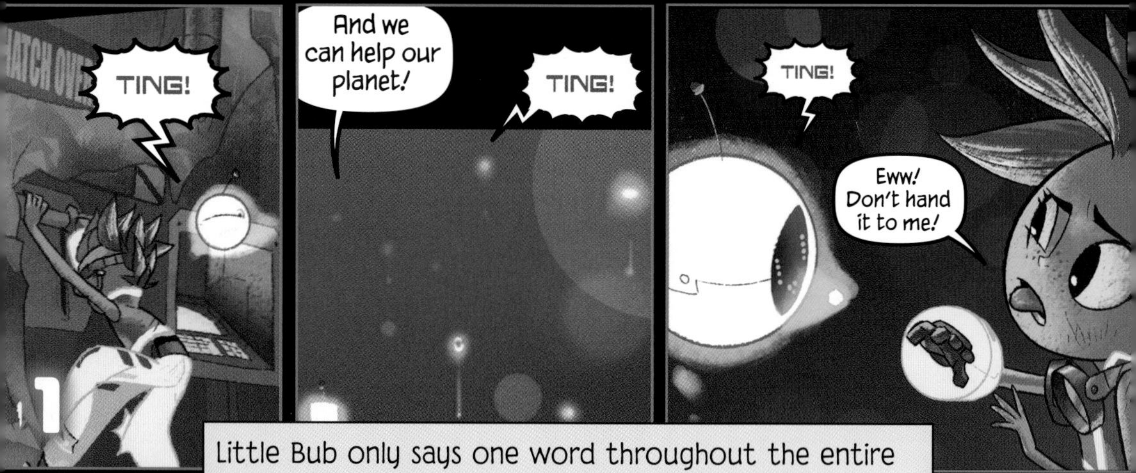
TING!
And we can help our planet!
TING!
TING!
Eww! Don't hand it to me!

Little Bub only says one word throughout the entire book: "Ting." What are some ways it uses the word differently? What do you think it's saying in the panels?

2

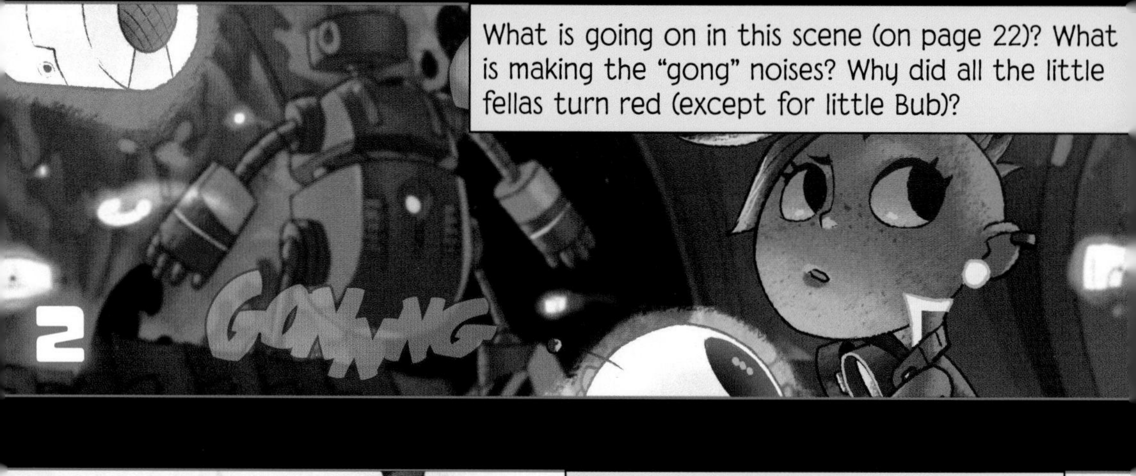

What is going on in this scene (on page 22)? What is making the "gong" noises? Why did all the little fellas turn red (except for little Bub)?

3

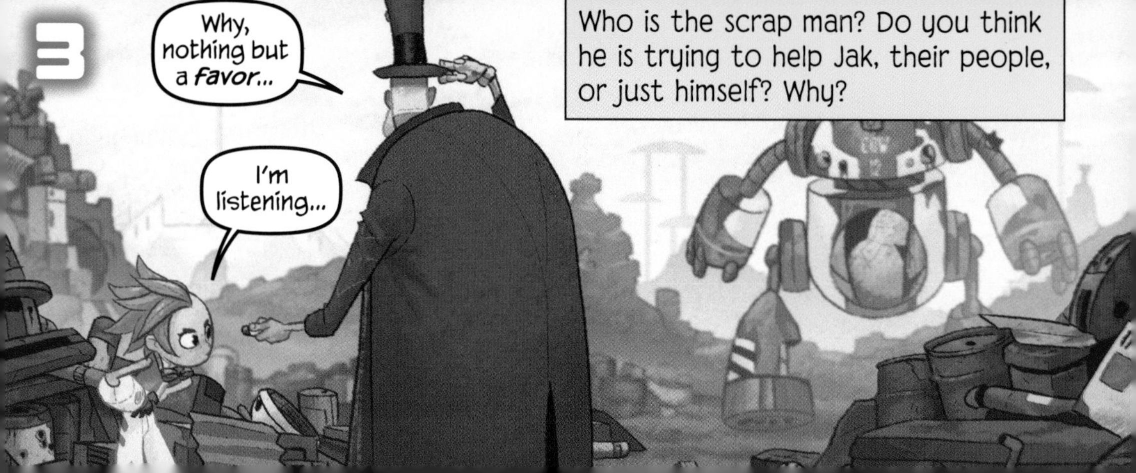
Why, nothing but a *favor*...
I'm listening...

Who is the scrap man? Do you think he is trying to help Jak, their people, or just himself? Why?

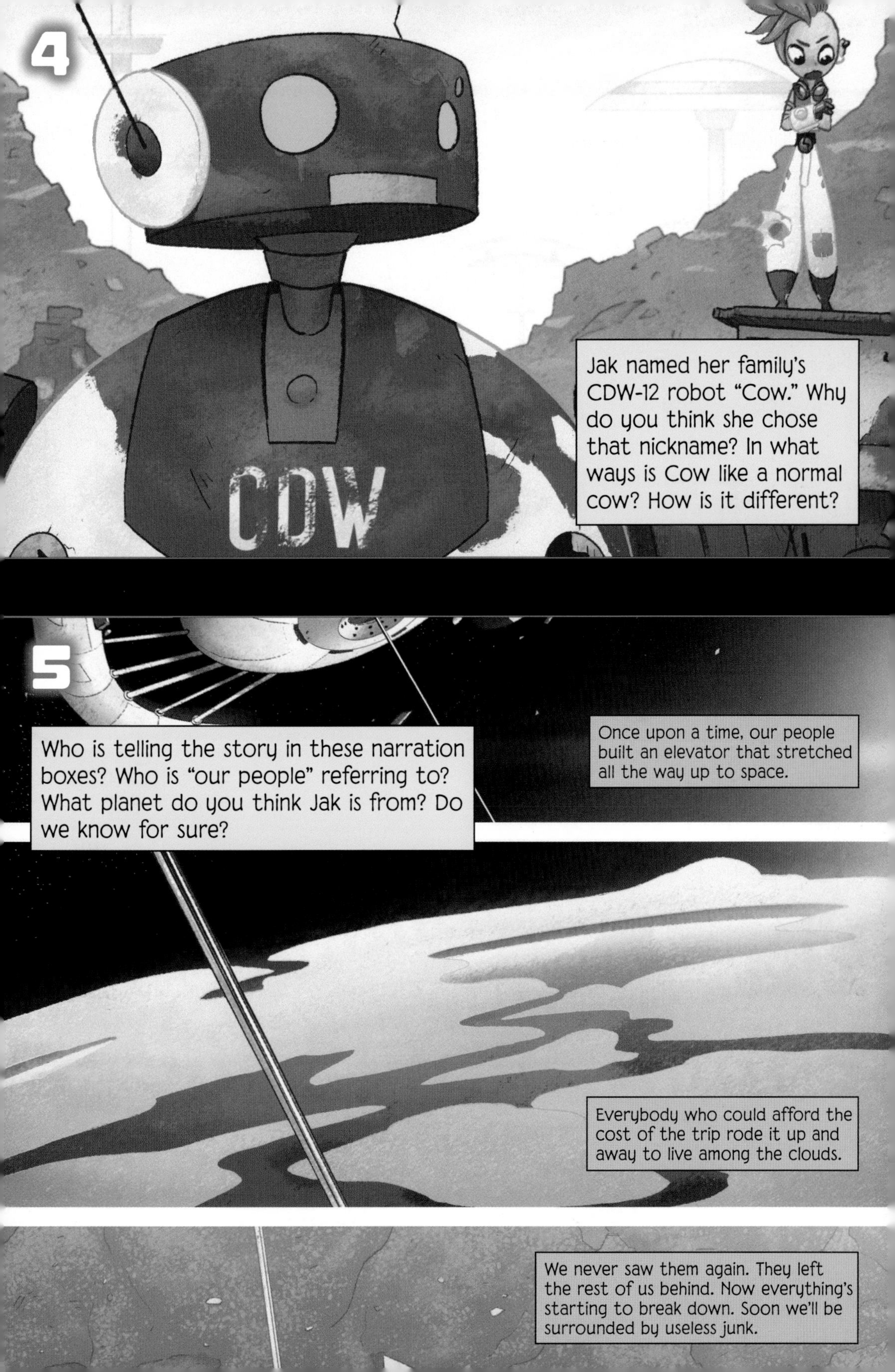
4
Jak named her family's CDW-12 robot "Cow." Why do you think she chose that nickname? In what ways is Cow like a normal cow? How is it different?
CDW
5
Who is telling the story in these narration boxes? Who is "our people" referring to? What planet do you think Jak is from? Do we know for sure?
Once upon a time, our people built an elevator that stretched all the way up to space.
Everybody who could afford the cost of the trip rode it up and away to live among the clouds.
We never saw them again. They left the rest of us behind. Now everything's starting to break down. Soon we'll be surrounded by useless junk.

AUTHOR

Carl Bowen is a writer, husband, and father living in Lawrenceville, Georgia. He has written several comic books for kids, including retellings of *20,000 Leagues Under the Sea* (by Jules Verne), *The Strange Case of Dr. Jekyll and Mr. Hyde* (by Robert Louis Stevenson), *The Jungle Book* (by Rudyard Kipling), "Aladdin and His Wonderful Lamp" (from A Thousand and One Nights), *Julius Caesar* (by William Shakespeare), and *The Murders in the Rue Morgue* (by Edgar Allan Poe). Carl's military fiction series of books called Shadow Squadron earned a star from Kirkus Book Reviews.

ILLUSTRATOR

Omar Lozano lives in Monterrey, Mexico. He has always been crazy for illustration and is constantly on the lookout for awesome things to draw. In his free time, he watches lots of movies, reads fantasy and sci-fi books, and draws! Omar has worked for Marvel, DC, IDW, Capstone, and several other publishing companies.

GLOSSARY

airlock (AIR-lock)--an airtight chamber with a controlled level of air pressure that provides (or prevents) access to a space with a different air pressure (like from inside a space station to outer space)

atmosphere (AT-muhss-feer)--a mass of gases that surround a planet or star

avatar (AV-uh-tahr)--a small picture that represents a computer user in a game, on the Internet, etc. The picture does not have to look very much (or at all) like the user.

marvels (MARH-vuhlz)--things that are amazing, wonderful, or extremely good

nanobots (NAN-oh-botz)--tiny, microscopic robots that some scientists believe will one day be able to replicate (create copies of themselves) in order to fix, repair, or upgrade technology

scrap (SKRAP)--a leftover, small piece of something after the main parts have been used. Scrapyards (places where scrap is left) often contain metal parts from vehicles, robots, and other forms of technology.

surrounded (suh-ROWN-did)--moved close to someone or something on all sides in order to stop someone or something from escaping

swarm (SWARM)--a very large number of things moving together as one, like a swarm of bees (or nanobots!)

useless (YOOS-liss)--broken, or not producing or able to produce the effect you want

AWESOMELY EVER AFTER.

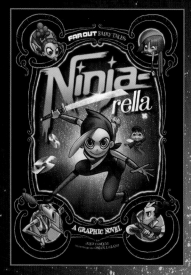

FAR OUT FAIRY TALES

ONLY FROM CAPSTONE!